MW00399717

Mystery novelist Hazel Martin's maid suspects foul play when her childhood friend Doris jumps from the third-story turret of Farnsworth Abbey. Unable to resist an investigation, especially one that's staged to look like suicide, Hazel calls in help from her chauffeur, her cook, and even the mysterious butler her husband hired before his death. Hazel soon learns that Doris's death was no accident. Someone had a secret, and they wanted to keep it that way.

With her trusty Siamese cat, Dickens, by her side and handsome Detective Chief Inspector Gibson at her disposal, Hazel follows a trail of clues to reveal a surprise twist that even the killer didn't suspect.

USA Today Bestselling Author Leighann Dobbs brings back the spirit of the Golden Age of mysteries in this classic whodunit set in the 1920s.

# MURDER BY MISUNDERSTANDING

## HAZEL MARTIN MYSTERIES BOOK 2

## LEIGHANN DOBBS

LEIGHANN DOBBS PUBLISHING

This is a work of fiction.

None of it is real. All names, places, and events are products of the author's imagination. Any resemblance to real names, places, or events are purely coincidental, and should not be construed as being real.

MURDER BY MISUNDERSTANDING

Copyright © 2017

Leighann Dobbs Publishing

http://www.leighanndobbs.com

All Rights Reserved.

❀ Created with Vellum

## CHAPTER ONE

From the way Dickens was acting, Hazel Martin should have known that murder was afoot.

The sleek Siamese cat paced the perimeter of the sitting room, his tail held high and his pale-blue eyes alert within the dark-brown mask of his face. Quite striking. And upsetting, truth be told. Dickens usually only acted that way when there was a suspicious death to be investigated.

Or when Alice, her cook, chased him with a broom.

This early, however, Alice was ensconced in the kitchen, baking and preparing items for the daily meals ahead. Hazel sniffed and detected a hint of warming yeast and frying bacon in the air. The first rays of the rising sun beamed through the window to Hazel's left, drenching her in light while she enjoyed a triangle of toast and her morning tea.

Hastings Manor was one of those old Regency-period gems, tucked away on a quiet country lane in Oxfordshire, from the two-story beige-brick Georgian exterior and crisp-white front door, to the well-manicured circular gravel driveway and the plethora of gabled dormers and balustrades. Hazel had lived in the nearly two-hundred-year-old-place her entire life, first with her parents, and later with her husband, Charles.

Now that her dear Charles had passed away, she lived in the big, drafty house alone. In the three years since her husband had died, she'd slowly made some changes, both to herself and her home.

First, her appearance. Never one to fuss with it too much—she was always so busy writing—she'd finally gotten around to having her long brown hair cut into a shorter, flattering bob style that was all the rage these days, though she'd left the brown color and the few scattered strands of grey the way they were. She'd worked hard for them and considered them a sign of all she'd been through and survived.

Hazel had also updated her wardrobe at last, from the somewhat frumpy housedresses and comfortable skirts she'd worn when Charles had been alive, to more modern sheath dresses and even a few flapper-style gowns for evening. In that vein, she'd chosen a lovely drop-waist floral frock in shades of blue and white, with a darker-blue grosgrain band around the hips and the hem. It had long sleeves and a high neckline, and the shop assistant had gone on and on about how the color brought out the peaches-and-cream in her complexion. Charles would've had kittens if he'd seen the price tag—chief detective inspectors didn't make huge salaries—but her inheritance more than covered the cost of this and the entire household, plus supported her as her mystery writing career gained readership, so why not splurge a bit?

Hazel glanced around the sitting room and smiled. She'd designed this space to be her own private oasis, filled with books and mementos, lace and portraits of better days with her and Charles together. He'd been gone three years now, though she still missed him as if it were yesterday. There were also lots of knickknacks from her childhood—her favorite old china doll, Miss L, with her voluminous hoop dress; a papier-mâché bulldog pull toy; a small framed needlework piece she'd sewn when she was eight of two cats sewing while sitting on a chair.

"Good day, madam," her maid said, drawing Hazel back to the present. Maggie stood just inside the doorway to the small room, wringing her hands. Her brown hair was covered by a white cap to match her apron, and she wore a blue serge dress beneath. Her expression hovered between nervous and fearful, and her brown eyes were troubled.

Behind her stood Alice, ruddy faced from the heat of the ovens. She was several inches taller than Maggie and a good deal wider too. Her deepening frown spoke volumes. Something was definitely wrong this fine day. Hazel glanced at Dickens again and then, with a sigh, bid adieu to her peaceful morning and welcomed the two women inside.

"Please, ladies, come and sit." Hazel set her tea and the final edits on her latest mystery novel aside, gesturing toward the settee across from her. After she'd lost her dear husband, the long-standing servants had almost become Hazel's family now, and if something was bothering them, then it bothered her too. "You both look horribly upset. Tell me what's wrong."

Maggie and Alice took a seat on a lovely Victorian settee embroidered with red and pink roses, and Dickens, being Dickens, immediately ran over to flit about in Alice's skirts. The cook tried to shoo him away, but he persisted—as if he took the battle of wills between them as a personal affront.

The two had acted that way toward each other— Alice keeping her distance from the feline, Dickens having none of it—since the day Hazel had adopted the cat, though she suspected Alice was fonder of Dickens than she let on. The cook would never admit that, of course. Alice was stubborn through and through, most likely from her German heritage. She was also quite stocky and had no problem lifting and carrying the heavier pots and pans around the kitchen either—most likely also due to her stout German ancestors.

"Well, madam. You see, there's a bit of a problem, I'm afraid," Maggie said, stumbling over her words as the hand wringing continued. The girl seemed so innocent at times that Hazel was glad she was employed here at Hastings Manor, where scandalous, shocking things hardly ever happened. "I'm not sure how to say this."

"Just tell the truth, Maggie dear." Hazel gave her a sympathetic smile. The girl was young and always eager to help her with her investigations. The least Hazel could do was return the favor now. "That always works best."

Alice nudged Maggie in the side and gave her an urging look, cocking her head toward Hazel. "Tell her, Mags."

The maid nodded then frowned down at her hands, now clasped so tight in her lap that her knuckles were white. "It's my godmother's sister's daughter, madam." Maggie sniffled, and soon her thin shoulders shook with sobs. "You see, she died last night."

"Oh no." Hazel reached over and covered her maid's hands with hers. Alice put an arm around the girl and tucked Maggie into her side as well. "I'm so very sorry. What happened?"

"She fell," Maggie said, her voice hiccupping on a sob. "From a third-story window in the turret room at Farnsworth Abbey."

Stunned, Hazel blinked and sat back slightly. Farnsworth Abbey was a Jacobean country house much grander than Hastings Manor. It sat on several acres to the south of Oxfordshire, land that had been in the Wakefield family's name for centuries. To have a death like that at such a fine property was sure to draw all the wrong sorts of attention.

"They're saying it's suicide, madam." Maggie bit back another sob, her face scrunched with grief and tears. "But I know Doris would never kill herself. I know that because that's what happened to her mother, and she swore to me she'd never do that to herself. She's a good girl, Doris is."

Hazel exchanged a glance with Alice before continuing. "Did you know her well then?"

"We grew up together, were best friends when we were young. And I was there at her mother's funeral too, saw how deeply the death affected Doris. That's why I'm so adamant that she'd never, ever kill herself. It went against everything she believed."

"Right." Hazel patted the maid's hand then sat back in her seat, frowning. "Well, if it wasn't suicide, then it had to be an accident or murder."

At the mention of that word, Dickens meowed.

"If it was an accident, then that should come to light quickly during the police investigation. But if there were nefarious acts committed against your friend Doris," Hazel continued, giving a curt nod, "then I will help discover the truth."

"Oh, I appreciate the offer, madam" Maggie said, swiping the back of her hand across her wet cheeks. "But I know you're busy with your book, and the police have the area closed off already, and—"

"Nonsense." Hazel waved her hand dismissively. "I'll have made good progress with my editing by midmorning, and there's nothing like digging into a real-life murder to give me inspiration for the next novel, which I'm just starting." She frowned, picking up her jade Radite Sheaffer pen from the tooled leather case that held her personal collection of fountain pens, and a blank sheet of paper to jot notes from what Maggie had told her. "Though we can't assume it's murder just yet, I suppose."

The maid started to cry again, and Hazel placed a comforting hand on her knee.

"Now, Maggie," she said, keeping her tone quiet and soothing, "please understand. Most people don't want to believe their loved one could kill themselves, and you're no different. From what you've told me about Doris's mother, however, it does seem unlikely. How about if I pay a visit to Lord and Lady Wakefield at Farnsworth this afternoon and find out more about what happened?"

For the first time since entering the sitting room, Maggie smiled, albeit a sad one. "Thank you, madam. I'd be ever so grateful."

"Then that's what I'll do."

Hazel waited until Alice bustled Maggie from the sitting room, with the promise of fresh tea and biscuits in the kitchen, before picking up her editing again. Paying such a visit to the Wakefields' estate without it looking as if she were another gawker, there to see the gruesome scene, would be tricky. She'd need a solid plan of action and a bit of time to prepare.

Good thing Hazel knew exactly what to do and had time to implement her plan.

# CHAPTER TWO

That afternoon, Hazel bumped along in the back seat of her maroon Sunbeam Tourer with the black cloth top and white sidewall tires as her chauffeur, Duffy, headed toward Farnsworth Abbey. He was a handsome young chap, with his blond hair and sunny disposition. Enterprising too, from what she'd seen. He always seemed to be looking for other ways to help around the house when he wasn't driving her around. In many ways, he reminded Hazel of her Charles.

Normally, Hazel preferred the two-seater Resta for running her errands, but for visiting the stately Farnsworth Abbey, this vehicle seemed more appropriate. Charles had loved this car too, insisting on buying it even though it was too large for just the two of them. Even more so now that she was alone. But she did so love the rich quilted leather seats, dyed to match the exact color of the exterior, the dark paneling on the doors, and the sparkling silver trim. He'd originally wanted the Resta as their sole transportation, but they'd later decided on the five-seater model too, thinking they'd need room for the children someday. Except those children never came. Now it was just her, trying to get along as best she could.

Hazel sighed and stared out the window at the passing countryside.

Even after a sunny morning, the early-autumn air was still chilly. She adjusted her new floral brocade coat and patted the berry-colored cloche hat on her head. The milliner had claimed the shade complemented her chestnut hair and helped hide the glimmer of grey in the strands. It also picked up the color of the tiny crimson centers of the flowers on her coat and made her feel spiffy at the same time. A win all around in her book.

Still, with the briskness in the air, it certainly felt as if winter might come early that year to Oxfordshire, and she was glad for her new thick coat and the matching set of kidskin leather gloves. The trees had all turned, and leaves were scattered everywhere on the ground, blown to and fro by the wind and the car's whirling tires. They hit several bumps in the road, and Hazel bounced slightly on the seat.

A few minutes later, Duffy pulled up in front of the sprawling grand house and parked. It held all the hallmarks of the architectural style, including lots of columns and pilasters surrounding the entrance, and the usual Jacobean decorative flourishes—scrolls, strapwork, and diamond-shaped lozenges—decorating the redbrick exterior.

Duffy jogged around the car quickly to open Hazel's door for her then bowed slightly as he took her hand to help her down. The mischievous look in his green eyes always made Hazel wonder what he got up to when he wasn't chauffeuring her around.

"I'll be back in an hour, madam, as you requested." He tipped his black hat to her then got back behind the wheel and took off back down the gravel drive.

Hazel walked up to the massive entry door and knocked, using the golden lion's head knocker. Where her home, Hastings Manor, was small enough to feel cozy, Farnsworth Abbey was gigantic—the kind of place with dozens of rooms, stables with horses, several cars, and multiple butlers, cooks, chauffeurs, and maids. There was a wing for the staff, another wing for the family, and the center part of the house where the two mingled.

Moments later, the door opened and an older gentleman dressed in formal livery bowed to her, inviting her inside. A flutter of butterflies swarmed through Hazel's stomach. She'd visited Lord and Lady Wakefield on several occasions but didn't know them terribly well. In addition to them, the family included their twins, Eugenia and Thomas, both tall and in their midtwenties.

Hazel gazed around the gorgeous oak-paneled main hall of the home, the carved wooden staircase leading up to the second floor, the vaulted ceilings, and the stained-glass windows that dated back to the early seventeen hundreds.

"Right this way, Mrs. Martin," the butler said after taking her coat. He ushered her into a large, elaborate drawing room lined with sculptures and tapestries, where Eugenia sat sobbing with her brother, Thomas, at her side, trying to console her. Both had inherited the pale skin and freckles of their lineage, though Eugenia's hair was more of a light blond, whereas Thomas's had more of a red tinge.

Across from them was Lady Wakefield, her writing desk mounded with papers. Lord Wakefield read the newspaper before a crackling fire, ignoring them all. It seemed great wealth did not necessarily go hand in hand with great warmth. He wore black-rimmed reading glasses, and his hair was salt-and-pepper grey now, the color contrasting with his burgundy smoking jacket. His dark brows were knit, as if he was concentrating hard on his reading material. His pipe billowed a constant stream of smoke, scenting the air with the fragrance of tobacco and vanilla.

"Oh, Mrs. Martin," Lady Wakefield said, waving her over. She stood a bit taller than Hazel and had a rigid set to her shoulders that bespoke old money and tight restraint. Her auburn hair was clipped back in a low chignon, and her peach-colored dress and pearls highlighted the inquisitive sparkle in her hazel eyes. "I'm so glad to see someone who isn't a police officer."

"Please, call me Hazel." She looked quizzically at the teetering stack of unopened mail, packages, and parcels on the desk. "And if it's a bad time, I can return later."

"No, no. Not at all," Lady Wakefield said, directing Hazel farther into the room. The dappled sunlight through the large windows along one side of the room helped ease the cloistered feeling of the space. "Please don't mind my mess. I personally open all the post when it's delivered each day. You just caught me right after the postman came, that's all." She placed her hand over a mound of letters and moved them away from the edge. "With our family going back to the time of Henry the Eighth, I feel we have a social responsibility to promptly handle our correspondence ourselves instead of leaving it to the staff."

Eugenia gave a loud sniffle, and Lady Wakefield glanced at her daughter then back to Hazel. "I'm sure you've heard the tragic news by now. With poor Doris being Eugenia's lady's maid, the two were very close. The horrible incident is too bad, really. Though I did warn my daughter not to get too attached to the servants." She cast a disapproving stare toward her children. "This is what happens when you treat the staff like family."

Hazel bristled a bit under the comment. That was exactly how she saw her household staff and wondered if Lady Wakefield would disapprove of her as well for it. Most likely, but at this point, Hazel didn't care. She was much too busy with her books to get out and socialize much, and after losing Charles, she had no desire to live the high life that many younger socialites enjoyed. Give her a great novel, a good brandy, and a toasty fire, and she was happy.

"Such a scandal," Lady Wakefield continued, giving a sullen tsk. "And all over the papers already too. I just hope it doesn't mar the family name." She gave her recalcitrant husband a stern look. "We have a guest, dear. Don't be rude."

Lord Wakefield glanced up at Hazel over the top

of his newspaper and gave a short grunt by way of acknowledgement then went back to his reading.

*Right then.*

"As I said, so very nice to have you visit us today, Hazel," Lady Wakefield said, ignoring her husband's social laziness. "What brings you to Farnsworth Abbey this afternoon?"

"I wanted to stop by and offer my condolences for your troubles." She narrowed her gaze on a priceless portrait of one of Lord Wakefield's illustrious ancestors hanging above the fireplace. Beside it stood busts of the original Lord and Lady Wakefield, and nearby hung the Wakefield family crest. "Shocking as it sounds, I just so happen to be writing a book about someone falling from a third-floor window for my next novel. You wouldn't think it too morbid of me if I asked to see the room from which Doris fell, would you? For research purposes, of course."

Lady Wakefield blanched, quickly moving from behind the desk to take Hazel by the arm and tug her back out into the hallway. Confused, Hazel followed behind her. Had she stepped in it already without realizing it? "I'm so sorry, did I say something amiss?"

"No, no." Lady Wakefield glanced back into the drawing room before looking down the bridge of her beaklike nose at Hazel. "It's just all this is still so disturbing for poor Eugenia. We don't like to talk about it in front of her. She's so delicate, you know."

"Oh dear. Please forgive me," Hazel said. "I'm sure it must be awful for all of you, knowing what happened upstairs. What with a young girl like that jumping for no reason." Hazel shook her head and frowned. "So terribly tragic. And so unexpected. Was there a fight or any indication she might've been planning it? Perhaps trouble with another staff member?"

"Perhaps. I don't really know." She pulled Hazel a bit farther away from the drawing room door before continuing. "Though I suspect there might've been some trouble amongst the staff, yes. From what the housekeeper told me, Doris seemed sad and out of sorts lately, but everything else was going along, and she was performing her duties adequately, so I let it drop.

"The night it happened, we'd had a lovely supper too, then my husband retired to his study, and I went to my sewing room, as we often do on Thursday nights. Our rooms are just across the hall from each other in the family's private wing. I have my sewing table set up so I can see into the mirror on the wall and see into his study. Anyway, I was just finishing a lovely evening shawl when I heard the scream." She shuddered and looked away. "Would you like to see it? It's quite beautiful."

It took Hazel a moment to realize the woman was talking about the shawl and not the scream. Hoping to get a look at the crime scene, she took Lady Wakefield up on the offer. "Oh, yes, please. I so admire those with excellent needlework skills. I've never had the patience for it myself."

"It relaxes me, helps take my mind off the problems of running such a large estate and raising a family. What a lovely hat you have on today, by the way." Lady Wakefield led her deeper into the home, past the enormous state dining room, then the elegant library, then into the family's private wing and to the study and sewing rooms. She walked around a large oak table and opened a drawer in the mahogany credenza against the wall, pulling out the shawl. Hazel did have to admit it was lovely—pale-pink silk embroidered with delicate roses and edged with long tassels.

"It's beautiful. What talent you have with a needle and thread." Lady Wakefield beamed under the compliments while Hazel's mind raced, looking for clues about Doris's death. "I made a small sampler once, when I was a child, but nothing like this."

"You flatter me, Hazel." Lady Wakefield smiled, stroking the fine fabric reverently. "This exquisite silk came all the way from Paris, you know. I was lucky enough to find it at Miss Pinkerton's shop last Wednesday. I'd timed my visit just right too because they'd just received their weekly delivery by train. The station's just across the road, and I could even see the train pulling out through the shop window. I was there when Miss Pinkerton opened the box. Otherwise, someone else would have grabbed it, I'm sure."

"Yes, that's very fortuitous indeed," Hazel said, distracted. She needed to steer this conversation toward Doris again. "I've just finished a book earlier today. Did I mention I'm starting a new one about a third-floor jumper?"

Lady Wakefield's smile faded, and she refolded the shawl, placing it atop her sewing table before facing Hazel again. "Yes, you mentioned it."

"Could I possibly see the turret room now?" she asked, now that they were out of Eugenia's earshot. "It would help me ever so much with my research."

"I don't know," Lady Wakefield said, her tone reluctant, and Hazel's hopes fell. "We don't normally allow guests up into that part of the house. It's quite old and musty."

But desperate times called for desperate measures.

"Of course, I'd certainly mention you and your family in my acknowledgments."

"Our family name, mentioned in a mystery novel?"

"Whatever you prefer. My books are becoming quite popular. It would be seen by many people." Her voice rose slightly over the last few words, playing to the woman's self-importance.

"Being named in a novel is quite an accomplishment, from what I've been told. Many of the great old families are doing it these days."

Lady Wakefield frowned. "I just don't know. I'm worried enough about our name being associated with such a nasty event. Suicide." She whispered the word carefully, as if it might taint her. "I'd hate for the scandal to become worse than it already is."

"Oh, there'll be no mention of that in my book, I assure you," Hazel said, patting the woman's hand. "After all, we're not even sure that's what happened to Doris."

"Oh, I'm sure she took her own life," Lady Wakefield said, her tone shocked. "Whatever else could it be?"

"Indeed," Hazel said, walking over to a wall of ribbons and trim, running her fingers over the lace and silk, all neatly color-coded, giving Lady Wakefield a chance to mull things over. "Whatever else could it be?"

"Well," she said at last, "I suppose it couldn't hurt

anything. And a mention in one of your popular books might do wonders for my Eugenia's marital prospects too." She moved to the door and leaned out into the hall. "Mrs. Crosby?"

Soon, a housekeeper arrived, and Lady Wakefield walked the older, grey-haired woman over to Hazel. "Mrs. Crosby, this is Hazel Martin, our guest. Please escort her up to the turret room."

---

"RIGHT THIS WAY, MA'AM," Mrs. Crosby said, leading Hazel back through the grand dining room and center of the house and over to the staff wing, into the kitchen, to a back staircase leading upstairs to the third-floor turret room. Every so often, Hazel caught the woman glancing back at her, as if she wanted to say something then reconsidered. The woman's wire-rimmed spectacles gave her a studious air, and her plump frame reminded Hazel a bit of Alice.

The stairs were narrow, and the air smelled musty, as if the area wasn't used much, just as Lady Wakefield had indicated. At the top of the stairs was another short hallway with two doors—one at the far end of the hall and one in the middle. Mrs. Crosby walked to the middle door. "This way, madam."

As she followed the housekeeper, Hazel couldn't help wondering where that other door led. Another set of stairs, perhaps? An escape route? Yet another wing of this enormous mansion?

Hazel followed the housekeeper inside the turret room and found another space that looked as if it didn't get much use. There was a small twin-sized bed with a bare striped mattress and a child-sized bureau with a thick coating of dust against one wall. The space was narrow and cramped and held no other furniture, or anything else, for that matter. Hard to imagine why Doris, or anyone else, would come up here. The girl could've been meeting someone, she supposed, but the gloomy atmosphere was hardly romantic. Maybe another sort of meeting? To exchange information or hold a conversation outside the prying ears of the rest of the staff?

One dirty window in the far wall looked out over the home's roofline. Hazel peered out to the left and saw a narrow ledge of parapet covered in metal flashing leading from the window to the roof. Two sets of deep, long scratches marred the edge of the flashing. Beside them was a small tuft of black fur blowing in the breeze.

She filed away the information for later then turned to face the housekeeper again. "Mrs. Crosby, why do you think Doris was up here? Was it part of her duties to clean this area, or was it something else?"

The housekeeper eyed the filthy dresser and snorted. "She most certainly was not cleaning, that's for sure. Not with all this dust and grime. No. I think it's quite obvious why the girl came here. To jump."

"Really?" Hazel crossed her arms to keep warm. The room had a definite chill, both literal and figurative. "So Doris was depressed then?"

"Oh, well." Mrs. Crosby looked away, her eyes lowered. "It's not really my place to say."

"But if it was?"

The older woman held Hazel's gaze a moment, a slight flush staining her pale, wrinkled cheeks. "Well, if it was, I'd say that our Miss Doris was a little too fast and loose with her affections and that's what got her into trouble. Wouldn't be surprised if she had more than one lover too." On a roll now, Mrs. Crosby stepped closer, her expression conspiratorial. "Don't mind telling you that Doris was anxious lately too, like she might've been mixed up in something she shouldn't have been. My theory is she was despondent over having to choose between her men."

"Her men?"

At Hazel's alarmed look, the housekeeper seemed to catch herself and stepped back, smoothing a hand down the front of her grey apron and schooling her features back into stoicism. "I don't want to talk out of turn, Mrs. Martin, but I did warn Lady Wakefield about what I saw going on with Doris. So when she jumped, Lady Wakefield pulled me aside and said that it was understandable, given the circumstances I'd shared with her and that's most certainly why Doris jumped. She even gave me permission to tell the police as much too."

"I see." Hazel pushed away from the wall. "You truly believe that Doris killed herself then?"

"I do," Mrs. Crosby said, giving her an odd look. "What else would've happened?"

"Yes, what else?"

As they turned to leave, a fluffy black cat appeared at the top of the stairs. The feline sat there, regal as a monarch, watching Hazel with an unwavering green gaze as if trying to tell her something. Given Dickens's penchant for predicting murders, Hazel didn't take her feline forecasts lightly.

The housekeeper noticed her staring at the cat and gave a dismissive wave, her tone disapproving. "Oh, that's just Norwich. He's Miss Eugenia's cat. Always getting up to shenanigans. In fact, Doris was the one who'd chase after him each time he got away. He's not allowed outside, what with all of Lady Wakefield's birds in the garden. Lord help us all when Norwich catches one. He likes to leave their little heads in the big hall for Lady Wakefield to find. She nearly passed out the last time it happened. Not sure how he escaped the house or her wrath, but he always seems to find a way."

"Hmm." Hazel gave the cat a wink and a smile. Norwich twitched his tail and purred. "He seems like a good boy to me."

"Good boy?" Mrs. Crosby scoffed. "Poor Doris was always chasing after him. Climbing up on the gazebo roof or extracting him from a tree. I told her she should focus on her own work, helping Miss Eugenia, and stop focusing so much on that nuisance cat, but she never did listen." She pursed her lips. "Turns out the creature must have been fond of her. Saw her off to whatever comes next in a way."

"How so?" Hazel frowned.

"He's the first one who showed up on the scene downstairs after Doris jumped."

"Really?" Seizing the opportunity to learn more, Hazel asked as they descended the stairs, "What exactly happened the night Doris died?"

"Well, let's see. It was shortly after supper when I heard the scream from upstairs. I was in the dining room, doing the final clearing. All of a sudden there were footsteps thundering on polished floorboards as people ran up to the turret room to see what was going on. It's a bit of a distance, as you can see, so it was quite a ruckus. I saw Betsy, the housemaid, run past the dining room door, so I decided to go up too. Granted, I'm a bit slower than the rest of them, though, so by the time I made it to the top of the stairs, it was already over. Lady Wakefield was standing there, her face white as a ghost, poor thing."

"Wait." Hazel stopped. "Lady Wakefield was in the room when Doris jumped?"

"No," Mrs. Crosby said. "As far as I know, Doris was alone in the turret room. Lady Wakefield had just heard the screams like the rest of us and hurried to see what had happened."

"Hmm." Hazel continued through the maze of hallways, compiling a list of suspects as she went. "Who else was present when you got to the third floor?"

"Mr. Donovan, our estate manager. Betsy, as I mentioned. There was also George the under-butler, and Harrison the butler too. Master Thomas followed behind me up the stairs."

"And what did you all see when you walked into the turret room?"

"The open window. And then when you peered out..." The housekeeper's face greyed. "Well, it was just awful. As soon as it was apparent she'd jumped, we all ran downstairs to the ground floor. The rest of the staff had started to gather around Doris's body too by then. She'd fallen so far and landed so hard, there was nothing anyone could do to save her by then, poor thing." Her voice trailed off, and her gaze lowered. "Miss Eugenia was in her room and had just run outside to see what all the commotion was about, but we herded her back inside and sat her down in the drawing room. She's much too delicate to see such gruesome things. She and Doris were very close too, though I never understood why."

The whole thing sounded far too near to a plot in one of Hazel's mystery novels for her comfort. She frowned. "So most of the household were here and the staff were on duty when Doris died and either were in the room where she jumped or downstairs near her body after the fact?"

Mrs. Crosby scowled. "I suppose that's right, yes. Though a few were missing. The chauffeur and the stable boys weren't there. Neither was the cook, as she was busy in the kitchen."

"What about Lord Wakefield?"

"No. He wasn't there either."

They reached the main part of the house again and walked back into the main hall.

"What happened after you got Miss Eugenia inside and into the drawing room?" Hazel asked.

"By then the police had arrived, of course. That handsome Detective Chief Inspector Gibson came." The housekeeper fluffed her grey hair. "Pretty sure he's coming back this afternoon too."

As if on cue, the doorbell rang, and Harrison, the butler, answered, letting Gibson into the main hall. Hazel's pulse quickened, and heat flushed her cheeks. He was handsome, no lie there, with his dark hair and eyes and athletic build. And yes, they'd worked together to solve his last case. She'd had fun and had been fairly sure he did too. But then Alice had gotten it into her head to encourage Gibson to court Hazel, and Hazel really wasn't ready for that and... *blast.* She'd been so busy ogling the man she'd forgotten to hide.

Gibson spotted her and smiled, heading down the hall toward where she and Mrs. Crosby stood. Hazel tried to duck into a nearby doorway to avoid him, but it was too late.

"Hazel, always a pleasure to see you again," Inspector Gibson said, his kind brown eyes twinkling with amusement, as if he knew exactly what she'd been trying to do, namely duck his company. "You're looking well."

Hazel took a deep breath and smoothed a hand down the front of her dress before meeting his gaze, praying she didn't look as flustered as she felt. "Inspector Gibson. Very nice to see you again as well."

He smiled, his teeth even and white against his tanned skin. "Please excuse me if I'm mistaken, but I believe we agreed to be on a first name basis after our last encounter."

Fresh heat prickled her cheeks, and the nosy housekeeper's stare weighed heavily on her shoulders. He would have to bring *that* up. She swallowed hard and nodded. "You're correct. Michael."

"Always good to hear, Hazel." His smile widened, showing an attractive dimple on the right side, though she detected a hint of suspicion in his gaze. "What brings you to Farnsworth Abbey today? You aren't getting involved in the nasty business about Doris, I hope."

"Of course not," she said. He was well aware she'd lent a hand in her late husband's investigations when he'd been chief inspector. Writing mystery novels had given Hazel a keen sense of intrigue and above-average deduction skills, and Charles had appreciated her talents. Why, he'd even credited her as a consultant at times.

Still, she wasn't sure there was anything to investigate about poor Doris yet, and the last thing she wanted was for Michael Gibson to know she was there on the request of her maid, so instead she came up with what she hoped was a plausible excuse. "I just came to visit my friend, Lady Wakefield. Now, if you'll excuse me."

Hazel brushed past him and headed for the front door with as much pride as she could muster. Grabbing her coat from the butler, who had scrambled to retrieve it at her hasty departure, she prayed Duffy would have the car ready and waiting on the front steps so she didn't embarrass herself further by twiddling her thumbs while Inspector Gibson watched.

---

## CHAPTER THREE

"May I take your coat, madam?" Hazel's butler, Shrewsbury, asked once she'd arrived back at Hastings Manor again. "Wise choice to dress warmly. It's chilly out, and you wouldn't want to catch cold."

"Yes, thank you." She stopped in the main hall and allowed him to help her out of the heavy, fur-trimmed wool. Shrewsbury, now in his midfifties, had been hired by Charles and now looked after her like a fussy mother hen since her husband's passing. She'd often wondered if Shrewsbury's duties had run to far more than that of a normal butler—what with all his unusual associates stopping by the house at all hours of the day and night and his mysterious trips to visit family members he'd never mentioned before—but the man was an excellent butler, and Hazel felt completely safe and secure with him in the house, so she never questioned him.

"Another murder, madam?" he asked as he hung her coat in the side cupboard then faced her, his grey brows knit above his disapproving stare. There was, however, a slight smile on his lips, which took away any true censure. Given how often he helped her, the wily butler enjoyed her cases as much as she did, she was sure.

Hazel pulled off her gloves and handed them to him, leaving her cloche hat on for now. It was such a pretty burgundy shade, and she did feel so young and pretty in it. Even Lady Wakefield had commented on it, which made her happy. "If you must know, yes. After visiting with the Wakefields, I do believe there's a matter of interest in the story."

"Very good, madam." Shrewsbury gave her a slight bow then walked with her into the sitting room. "I heard how you helped Mrs. Pembroke this summer while I was tending to my brother. Charles would've been proud, ma'am."

"Thank you." Hazel's heart pinched from his compliment. Coming from the staid, enigmatic butler, it meant a lot. She took a seat in her favorite chair by the window once more. The beveled glass looked so pretty this time of day, the sun's rays filtering through the edges like a prism, casting rainbows across the floor. "Could you fetch Alice and Maggie for me, please?"

"Certainly, madam," Shrewsbury said, bowing once more before leaving the tiny room.

While she waited, Hazel straightened the pages of her latest manuscript and wondered if Charles would have indeed been proud of her.

She used to help him on his cases, and it had been something she really enjoyed. Those investigations also helped her with her novels. As did her husband. In fact, her dear Charles had been such a big help to her, that with this last book—her first without him— she'd been afraid she might not be able to complete it on her own.

As she stacked the last of the papers, Hazel smiled. She'd done it, though, finished the book. And by doing so had gained more confidence in her detecting skills. Plus, Shrewsbury had been right. She had helped solve Myrtle Pembroke's case. Yes. Charles would have been proud of her, and maybe, just maybe, he was looking on her with a smile.

"You wished to see us, madam?" Maggie asked as she and Alice stood in the sitting room doorway.

"Yes." Hazel waved them in. "Please have a seat."

Once the ladies had settled themselves on the

settee in front of her, Hazel continued. Both wore starched white aprons and matching white caps, though Alice's dress underneath was blue, while Maggie's was a light-green cotton. "As you know, I went to Farnsworth Abbey this afternoon to inquire about poor Doris. And I'm afraid that there may be some truth to Maggie's assertion that this wasn't a suicide."

The young maid gasped. "So you *do* think she was murdered?"

"I'm not sure I'm ready to go that far yet, Maggie." Hazel reached down to stroke Dickens, who'd slinked into the room as they talked. The large silver-beige cat stretched into her stroking, back arched and tail high as he purred loudly. "But there are some suspicious circumstances to the story that warrant further investigation, I think."

Dickens ran across the space separating Hazel's chair from the settee and immediately began twining himself around Alice's ankles. Absently, the older cook bent to pet him, frowning. "You're going to investigate the death then, madam?" Alice asked.

"With Maggie's permission, of course." She smiled at her maid then gave Alice a look. "Seems as if Dickens is growing on you."

The cook straightened fast, scoffing and clasping

her hands in her lap. "He's all right, I suppose. As long as he stays out of my kitchen."

"You really think there might be something suspicious going on with the Wakefields?" Maggie asked, her eyes wide with interest. "Something involving my poor Doris?"

"Perhaps," Hazel said. "I saw some discrepancies while at Farnsworth Abbey and think it can't hurt to investigate them just to rule out any foul play."

"Then yes," Maggie said, her voice confident. "Doris is an old friend and deserves to have her name cleared."

"There is one more thing, though." Hazel leaned forward, her tone serious as she met her maid's gaze directly. "If I'm going to do this for you, I need you to be nothing but frank with me."

Maggie nodded. "Of course, madam."

"Good. Now tell me, was your friend Doris...*loose* with her attentions?"

"Loose?" The maid frowned.

"You know, did she flirt with a lot of men? Allow them certain...*liberties*?"

Cheeks flushing bright red, Maggie shook her head, her brown eyes wide with shock. "Oh no, madam. No. Doris was happy and fun loving, yes, but she was a good girl, Mrs. Martin. I swear."

"You and Doris were close then recently?" Hazel asked. "Spent a lot of time together?"

Maggie lowered her gaze, frowning. "Well, not exactly, madam. I mean we were thick as thieves back when we were young girls, but of late we've grown apart because of work and such. But even if I haven't seen her lately, I still know Doris wasn't loose. She would never do such things."

Hazel admired the girl's loyalty to her friend but wasn't entirely convinced. After all, no one wanted to believe awful things about their friends or family members. Maggie might believe her friend's reputation was above reproach, but that didn't make it true. In fact, Mrs. Crosby had seemed just as convinced of the opposite. That, along with the other inconsistencies in the stories, had Hazel certain there was more to the story of Doris's demise than a simple suicide. After all, in matters of love, passions could run high both in and out of the bedroom.

"All right, then. Thank you, ladies." Hazel smiled as the two women stood and headed toward the door. "I'll begin to look into things at my earliest convenience."

"Thank you, madam." Maggie curtsied and left.

"Dinner should be ready shortly, madam," Alice said, bowing slightly.

After the ladies left, Hazel patted her lap, and Dickens jumped up onto her knees. He sat with perfect posture, staring deeply into her eyes, his icy-blue gaze both wise and wary. She stroked his head and smiled. "Looks like you were right, Dickens. I do believe murder is afoot."

---

INSTEAD OF WORKING in the sitting room for the rest of the afternoon, Hazel decided to go up to the third floor of Hastings Manor and work from the sunny little writing room she'd set up there. It had a nice view outside over the gabled rooftop and parapets, much like the window Doris had fallen from. Dickens trailed behind her, grooming his paws while she chose from her selection of fountain pens for the day's tasks. A fresh buzz of inspiration bubbled inside her, and she wanted to harness it for her next book. Nothing like a real-life murder to get the creative juices flowing.

Picking up a Dubonnet-red Esterbrook, to match her jaunty cloche hat, Hazel settled in behind her small desk with her journal to begin plotting. After a minute, though, she switched pens to her old standby —a celluloid green Parker Duofold. It felt like a cherished friend in her ink-stained fingertips, and soon the ideas began to flow out onto paper. She sketched out a new location, new characters, a new world for them to operate within. This was her favorite part, when everything was crisp and new and the possibilities were endless.

Dickens jumped up onto the windowsill beside her to watch her write.

"Let's see, Dickens. What do we know so far about this Wakefield case?" She turned away from her novel's notes and started a new blank page, scribbling the name down at the top of the sheet, while Dickens meowed. "How about we start with conversations, eh?"

The cat flicked his plush tail.

"Right. Lord Wakefield seemed unaffected by the death, more interested in reading his newspaper than comforting his family," she wrote, talking aloud to her cat companion as she did so. "That's not unusual for a man of his stature, though. People of that station in life are normally so callous toward the staff. Not like us, eh." She reached over to scratch Dickens behind his ears. "We treat ours like family, don't we?"

Smiling, she went back to writing and musing. "But what if Lord Wakefield's indifference is *too* indifferent? Maybe he really isn't close with his family at all. Maybe he seeks his companionship elsewhere.

Maybe he was more familiar with Doris than he let on..." She tapped her pen against her lips, frowning. "If Doris really was loose, as Mrs. Crosby insinuated, then perhaps she was having an affair with Lord W."

Hazel suppressed a shudder. The man was no looker, that much was certain, but to each their own. She glanced over at Dickens, who was watching her with a lazy, half-lidded gaze. "Plenty of men in his position take advantage of the help, and Lord W is rich. If Doris was a gold-digger, she might have thought he could help her financially."

The cat purred, as if in agreement.

"And where was he when she fell? Lady Wakefield told me he stayed in his study instead of running upstairs like everyone else. Could he really be that unconcerned about the goings-on in the house that he didn't care?" Hazel shook her head. "Lady Wakefield, on the other hand, seemed upset enough for them both. And even more concerned about Doris's death tarnishing her family's name. Seems she cares more about appearances than actual facts surrounding the case. Their family tree might extend back to the Tudors, but a woman died on their premises. That needs to count for something."

Dickens yawned then flopped over on his side for a nap.

"And what about the twins? They seemed upset too." She remembered them huddled together on the settee in the drawing room, and memories of them as smaller children, always sticking up for one another, came to mind. She and Charles had gone over there for dinner a few times right after they'd been married. "Of course, they are twins too, which naturally makes them closer."

She toed off her shoes and stretched her legs out under the desk, relaxing. She'd already filled up two pages with notes, front and back, and started on a third. "And what about the servants? Maybe one of them is behind it all. Mrs. Crosby, the housekeeper, sounded like she disapproved of Doris. Her assessment of Doris is in direct contrast to what Maggie's told me about her friend, though. I need to get back in there and speak with some of the others to get their side of the story. Not sure how yet, though."

The cat meowed again, and Hazel glanced over, the view of the rooftop leading her to think about poor Doris again. Such a horrible way to die. Hazel was no sissy when it came to heights, but thirty-plus feet was a long way to fall. And there was something else that bothered her too. "According to Mrs. Crosby, the scream came from the third floor. Which doesn't make sense if it was a suicide. Who jumps on purpose and then screams?"

Hazel got up and moved Dickens gently aside before opening the window and looking down. The cat meowed loudly again and scrambled off the sill, leaving a scratch on the wood in his haste. She gave a short laugh and watched as the cat hurried from the room, as if in a panic. Apparently, an open window this high up was too treacherous for his taste. Still, Hazel stared at the mark he'd left behind on the sill, the gouge reminding her of the scratches on the outside ledge at Farnsworth Abbey. She turned back around and leaned her hips against the sill.

"What if those were marks from Doris trying to hold on?" She mused out loud to herself. "Doris's nails could have left those marks too, if that were the case. And if she was trying to hold on and save herself, that makes jumping highly unlikely. But was it an accident then?"

She plopped back down into her seat, scowling. With Doris's body now under police custody, looking at the maid's fingers for signs of trauma would be virtually impossible. If only her Charles were still alive, she could ask him to check for her. As it was, it seemed she was going to need help on yet another case. Inspector Gibson would have access to all the information she needed, including the coroner's reports from Doris's autopsy, if she dared to work with him again.

It wasn't that she disliked Gibson. Quite the contrary, in fact. And that was what scared her the most. She wasn't ready for that kind of involvement again, not yet. Perhaps not ever. Things between her and Charles had been too special, too perfect. She doubted she'd ever find that kind of love and acceptance again.

However, in the interest of her case, she'd put her personal concerns aside.

Now, she just had to work out how to contact the Inspector again without it looking obvious.

---

## CHAPTER FOUR

A few hours later, Hazel went back downstairs to talk to the staff. They gathered in the kitchen, the hub of her large home. As she was just one person, many of the rooms at Hastings Manor sat dormant, but not this one. This room was her favorite. It was filled with familiar things from her childhood, and she took comfort from the sparkling black-and-white tile floors and gleaming copper jelly molds hanging from the walls. Yellow-glazed pottery mixing bowls lined the pine shelves of the large hutch against one wall, and dappled late-day sunlight broke through the clouds outside to stream in through the high-set windows.

They all sat around the huge butcher-block table in the center of the space—Maggie, Shrewsbury, Duffy, and Hazel—while Alice bustled about, making two Battenberg cakes. Why they needed two, Hazel had no idea, but Alice had insisted. At thirty-eight, Hazel had still managed to maintain her slim, girlish figure. That could change quickly if her cook insisted on whipping up a plethora of goodies each day. The air filled with the smells of vanilla and cocoa and a hint of strawberries, which Alice used to color half of the cakes.

Hazel sighed and smiled at her staff sitting around the table. "I'm sure you're all wondering why I've called you here."

The staff exchanged looks but remained silent.

"The truth is I need help on this new case I'm investigating. I can't ask anyone from my social circles, as I'm sure you understand. What I need is dirty gossip, the kind not found in drawing rooms and polite tea parties. Duffy"—she glanced at her chauffeur—"I know you're well-connected with the staff at other homes in the area, especially Farnsworth Abbey. I thought you might know something, seeing as you're related to half the people in our local town."

"Well, madam," he said, running a hand through his thick dark-blond hair. He'd removed his usual black hat indoors and looked even younger because of it. "As a matter of fact, my second cousin twice removed is the under-butler for the Wakefields. If you'd like, I'd be happy to pump him for information later at the pub."

Alice snorted, stirring together butter, sugar, flour, ground almonds, baking powder, eggs, vanilla, and almond extract in a large mixing bowl. "Listen to you, Duff. Talking like a young rake, going to pubs to gossip and getting up to no good. You should be careful who you associate with behind our backs. And don't go spreading a load of rumors about us, either. You'd do well to mind your friends and watch your back around those others."

Duffy gave the cook an annoyed stare. "Like you're one to talk, with all your secret baking for Inspector—"

"Hush!" Alice's gaze darted to Hazel before she turned around fast to scrape the cake-mix into four separate tins. She then started a second bowl of the mix, this time minus the almond extract but adding pink food coloring and fresh strawberries. "What I bake and whom I make it for are my business. Besides, I don't see you complaining when it comes time to stuff your face."

Ears perking, Hazel crossed her arms. "It is my business, though. Who exactly is the second cake for, Alice?"

Huffing, the cook set the yellow mixing bowl aside and wiped her hands on her apron as she turned to face Hazel once more. Her cheeks were ruddy, and the tiny grey hairs around her face, peeking out from beneath her white cap, curled around her face. She kept her gaze lowered as she spoke, her brows knitted and her expression sheepish. "It's for Detective Chief Inspector Gibson, madam. But before you go getting upset, please let me explain."

"The Chief Inspector?" Hazel sat back, gaze narrowed. She'd always been well aware of her cook's nurturing nature—especially given Alice had lost a child when she was younger and thus tended to mother those under her care. She'd even known Alice had taken a liking to Inspector Gibson and had been trying to get them together since the Pembroke case. But baking for the man was something else altogether. Baking implied a certain intimacy that Hazel was just not comfortable sharing with another person yet. And yes, she liked Gibson. He was a good detective and trustworthy too, but she wasn't ready for anything more, with him or anyone else. Charles had only been gone three years, and thoughts of a romantic involvement with another man made her dizzy. Of course, she did enjoy her friendship with Inspector Gibson, though, and it was nice to have someone she could discuss murder with—both in real life and for her books—but that was as far as it went for her.

The fact her cook had been deceitful and had gone behind Hazel's back to cultivate a more substantial relationship with the Inspector might have made another employer angry. Not Hazel, though, because she knew Alice only did it out of concern for Hazel. Still, she didn't appreciate or need the attempts. She cleared her throat and frowned. "I had no idea you baked for Inspector Gibson."

Alice sighed and swiped a flour-covered hand across the tip of her nose, leaving more streaks than it wiped away. "He's a bachelor with no one to bake for him, madam."

As if *that* should explain everything. Hazel crossed her arms and scoffed. "And how exactly does he get these treats you make for him? Don't tell me you bring them to him?"

"Sometimes." Alice shrugged, the color in her cheeks darkening. "He lives near to where a friend of mine cleans. I don't go out of my way to drop them off, just sometimes when it's on my way. The other times, Duff delivers them for me." She met Hazel's gaze at last, her grey eyes rife with contrition and a twinkle of mischief. "Maybe you could use this next cake to your advantage, though, madam."

"How so?" Hazel gave her driver an annoyed stare for being in cahoots on such a scheme then glanced back to the cook. "I really don't see how a cake is going to help me with Doris's murder."

"Deliver it to him yourself. It gives you a perfect excuse to socialize a bit with him and find out what the police know about this new case of yours."

Hazel shook her head, aghast. "You expect me to go to a man's house, detective or not, alone? I couldn't do that. Talk about a gossip mill." She exhaled slowly. Still, Alice was right. She did need to talk to Inspector Gibson—Michael—about Doris's fingertips to see if the police had noticed any strange marks or scars on them. And it *was* 1923. Society's rules about men and women being alone together were changing nearly as fast as the industrial revolution. Maybe she could drop off the cake without raising any untoward suspicions. Just a friendly gesture, nothing more. Besides, she could set him straight on any notions he might have about going behind her back to use her staff to get to her too. Bad enough he'd asked her out to dinner after the Pembroke case. She'd turned him down, of course, but still...

A tiny flicker of heat zipped through Hazel's chest. Not that dinner with the Inspector would be bad. Quite the contrary, really. He was intelligent and funny, and those kind brown eyes of his were lovely to look at too. But she wasn't ready for that. Not now. Maybe not ever.

"I happen to know," Alice said, turning back to her

baking tasks again, "that Detective Chief Inspector Gibson takes his tea at four p.m. like clockwork, and it's almost that time now." She popped the eight baking tins in the oven and set the timer. "By the time these are done, that should be perfect. You could even be back home in time for supper, unless he invites you to dine with him at his place."

"I most certainly will not be dining alone with Gibson. At his home or anywhere else." Hazel gave her matchmaking cook an irritated stare. "If I take this cake to him, it will be only to discuss the case, nothing more. Understand?"

"Very well, then." Alice huffed, shooing both Hazel and the newly arrived Dickens from the kitchen. "Now go and get ready. I'll let you know as soon as the cake is ready to go."

"Fine. And the rest of you, please keep your channels of communication open. Any information you can glean from the staff at Farnsworth Abbey could mean the difference between solving Doris's case or not." Hazel headed up to her room, Dickens hot on her heels, and a strange tingle of anticipation inside her. Much as she hated to admit it, talking to Michael really was the only way to find out what she needed to know about Doris. It was the next logical step in her investigation. That was why she'd agreed to take him Alice's cake.

Once in her bedroom, she changed out of her navy-blue day dress and red cloche hat and into a new dark-green silk chiffon knee-length dress with a high neckline in front and a slightly lower cowl drape in the back. The seamstress had said the color brought out the auburn highlights in her brown hair and made her complexion pop. Tiny seed pearls dyed the exact shade of the fabric covered the bodice in front, and the hemline was cut in the new handkerchief style to show off her trim ankles and matching green pumps.

As she assessed her reflection in the mirror, patting her finger-waved hair and touching up her lipstick, Hazel reminded herself that none of this was to impress Michael Gibson. It was because of her promise to herself to modernize her look, to get rid of the dowdy, decades-old outfits of her past, to increase her confidence. Charles would never have wanted her to lock herself away from the world and turn into an old frump. He'd loved getting dressed up and going out to dinner. This was her tribute to him then, a life well lived. She chose a smaller bi-corn green velvet hat to match her dress and fitted it jauntily over her brown hair.

Hazel squared her shoulders and forced a smile at

herself in the mirror that she didn't quite feel. Yup. Confidence. That was exactly what she needed to face Michael alone and get the information she needed. And if perchance he asked her out to dinner again, she'd just politely refuse, exactly as she had the last time. Yes, that was the trick. After grabbing her small cloth daytime reticule, she kissed Dickens goodbye on the head then headed downstairs to meet Duffy.

## CHAPTER FIVE

A t four o'clock sharp, Duffy pulled the Sunbeam to a halt in front of Detective Gibson's flat in Berkeley Street. Hazel swallowed hard against the lump of nervous tension in her throat and clutched the green tin that held Alice's Battenberg cake on her lap. All this fuss over a cake seemed silly, really, yet she couldn't seem to slow the frantic race of her heart.

Duffy got out and came around to open the door for Hazel. "Would you like me to wait here for you, madam?"

"Yes, please," she said, her tone higher than normal. She coughed and tried again. "Yes, please. I shouldn't be too long."

"Very good, madam." Duffy tipped his hat to her then smiled, his calmness putting her at ease. "I'll just pull around the corner then."

Hazel waited until he'd gone, then took a deep breath for courage before walking up to the front door of the squat red brick building. The neighborhood was quite working class, though clean and tidy, with freshly swept pavements and wrought-iron railings. She walked up the plain granite steps and knocked on the black painted door, absently fiddling with the collar of her floral wool coat while she balanced the cake tin against her hip.

An older woman, mid-sixties, answered. A wool shawl was clutched tight around her sturdy shoulders. "May I help you?"

"Yes, I'm here to see Detective Chief Inspector Gibson, please."

The woman eyed her for a moment, her wary expression slowly dissolving into a huge grin. "Oh, my goodness. I recognize you, from your picture on the back of all the detective books! You're that author who writes the mysteries, aren't you?"

A faint rush of heat stormed Hazel's cheeks over the flattery, and the fact Michael apparently owned her books. She gave a slight nod and a hesitant smile. "Yes, that's me."

"Please, please, come in. I'm Detective Chief Inspector Gibson's landlady." The woman waved her inside, the smell of lemonwood soap and lye stinging her nose as she passed into a drab hallway. "The Inspector will be chuffed to have you visit, I'm sure."

Hazel scanned the bland beige walls and plain polished floorboards, clasping the cook's cake in her hands, her reticule swinging from one wrist. "Um, I've not actually been here before. Which floor is the detective on again?"

"Michael!" the woman yelled up through the stairwell. Hazel winced at the woman's booming voice. Not exactly the way she'd have preferred to be announced. "You've got a visitor."

Seconds later, a door opened on the second floor, and Detective Gibson poked his head over the railing. His surprised expression soon gave way to a warm smile as he set eyes on Hazel and the green cake tin. "Mrs. Martin. I didn't expect any company this afternoon. To what do I owe this pleasure?"

She ignored the rush of butterflies in her stomach at his appearance—white shirtsleeves, sans jacket, the cotton material rolled up to reveal tanned, muscular forearms with just a light dusting of hair, and the top button open at the neck—and held up the tin. "Alice has made you a treat. I was in the area, so I offered to deliver it personally. May I come up?"

"Of course." He waited as she climbed the stairs to the second floor then took the cake from her hands, his grin bright and shiny as a new penny. "Ah, Mrs. Duprey. Such a lovely woman and an even better baker."

"Yes," Hazel said, a tad out of breath from her exertion and her nerves. She looked anywhere but at him and forced a shaky smile. "Alice is quite nice."

"I'll say." He stepped back to allow her into his flat, his kind brown eyes narrowing at the size of the large tin. "Though I'm afraid she must think I need to gain weight from the way she keeps sending these sugary confections. Not going to complain about such a lovely courier."

Hazel wasn't sure how to respond to that, so she didn't.

Instead, she walked into his flat, pleasantly surprised to find a neat, tidy abode. Far from the typical bachelor place she expected, it was well decorated and well furnished, with cozy leather furniture and a thick Persian rug on the floor before the brick fireplace crackling against the wall. The walls were the same beige as downstairs, but here they seemed warmer and homelier matching well with his earth-toned theme.

"May I take your coat?" Michael asked, setting the cake in the kitchen then returning to her side in the living room. "I'm sorry the place is such a mess. Like I said, I wasn't expecting visitors."

"Yes, thank you." She allowed him to slip the coat off her shoulders then watched as he hung it up on a brass coat rack near the door. From where she stood, he didn't need to gain any weight at all, or lose any either. In fact, he looked pretty perfect just the way he was. He turned back with a smile, and she looked away fast. "And your home is lovely."

"Ah, well, a bloke does what he can. Please, have a seat. Would you like some tea and a slice of this cake? There's no way I can eat it all myself, and I'd hate to see Alice's fine work go to waste."

She hadn't been planning on staying for tea, but she did need to talk to him about Doris's body. Turning down his offer seemed rude and pointless. After all, what was she supposed to do? Sit and stare at him while he ate? "Yes, all right." Hazel took a seat in one of the chairs near the fire and watched as the Inspector walked back into his small galley-style kitchen to serve up their cake. "I will admit I did have a slight ulterior motive in making this delivery."

Michael glanced up at her, his small smile amused. "I should have guessed."

"When you saw me earlier at Farnsworth Abbey, I wasn't just there to give condolences."

He nodded but didn't say anything, so she continued. "My maid, Maggie, was a personal friend of the unfortunate deceased, and she asked me to look into Doris's death. She doesn't believe it was a suicide. She claims Doris would never harm herself in such a manner."

"And what do you think?" Michael asked, pouring water into a teapot from the steaming kettle on his stove. "Do you think she did herself in?"

Hazel fussed with her handbag on her lap. "After speaking with the Wakefields and their staff, I have my doubts as well."

"Hmm." He placed two plates of cake, the tea pot and two teacups on a tray, with a strainer, teaspoons, milk and sugar, then rejoined her in the living room, placing their food on a small table between them before taking the chair opposite hers in front of the fire. "I see. And what led you to have these doubts?"

"From speaking with Maggie and also some of the staff at Farnsworth, things just don't seem to be adding up," Hazel said, stirring sugar into her tea. "I would like to ask you if the coroner found any signs of scratches or wounds on Doris's fingertips."

Michael looked up at her, halting mid-bite of his cake and sighing. "I suppose I do owe you one after the way you helped me with the Pembroke case. And

Charles always spoke highly of your detective skills. That's good enough for me." He shoved the piece of cake in his mouth, chewing slowly and swallowing before continuing. "And yes, Doris's fingertips were scraped, and several of her nails were broken too, as if she were trying to hold on."

"I see." Hazel sipped her tea then set her cup aside. "So you're investigating this as a murder?"

"Yes," Michael said, devouring another bite of cake. "I shouldn't be discussing it with you, but I suspect keeping you out of it now is futile."

She smiled at his resigned tone. Clever man. "Who are your suspects?"

"No one firm yet."

"As I mentioned, when I was with the Wakefields today, I spoke to some of the staff," she said, throwing him a bone from her investigation. "Mrs. Crosby, their housekeeper, seemed to think Doris was a bit of a floozy. Which, by the way, is the opposite of Maggie's opinion. But perhaps Lord Wakefield or Thomas might have been friendly with her. It wouldn't be uncommon for the aristocracy to get involved with a young, pretty female member of their staff."

"Well, if she was giving her favors to one of the family, it couldn't have been to Wakefield," Michael said, finishing off the last of his cake. "He was at his club when she fell."

"Really? That's odd." Hazel scrunched her nose. "I distinctly remember Lady Wakefield telling me the lord was in his study opposite her sewing room at the time Doris's scream was heard."

"Huh." Michael took a swig of his tea then frowned. "Could she have been mistaken?"

"I highly doubt it."

"Why would she lie then?"

"Not sure." Hazel sat back, smiling when Michael gestured toward her untouched piece of cake. She'd feared this conversation would be awkward, but speaking with him felt the opposite—comfortable, cozy, normal. In truth, Hazel had missed this. She'd loved those evenings when Charles would come home early from work and they'd sit before a fire in his study and discuss the latest details of one of his cases. "Please, help yourself to my piece of cake. I've got dinner waiting for me back at Hastings Manor when I get home."

"Okay then." He readily accepted her invitation and took a bite out of her slice of cake as well. "So back to the family lying."

"Perhaps Lady Wakefield wasn't lying, though," Hazel said. "Maybe Lord Wakefield was in his study.

Or maybe she just thought he was in there when he'd actually left. That room is on the first floor, and I remember there being French doors, so he could've sneaked out without her knowing."

"Doesn't make much sense." Michael frowned around a second bite of her cake. "Why would the man sneak out to go to his own club?"

"There's the question, eh?" Hazel said, watching him over the rim of her teacup.

"Well." He finished off the second slice of the draughts-board-pattern dessert then took the empty dishes back to the kitchen. "The one thing we know for sure is that according to the coroner's report, Doris must have jumped around ten to eight as she died immediately due to injuries sustained in her fall." Michael rinsed off the dishes then wiped his hands on a towel. "And that timing matches the witnesses' accounts of when they heard her scream and those people present on the ground afterward."

"That scream is the other thing that bothers me." Hazel stood and walked toward the coat rack to get her things. She didn't want to spend too much time in a bachelor's rooms alone. She might be thirty-eight and a widow, but tongues could still wag. "Who screams when they jump on purpose?"

"Another good question." Michael leaned a hip

against the kitchen sideboard and smiled. "See? Charles was right. You are a clever one. Looks like this might be a murder after all."

"Yes, it does." Hazel slipped back into her coat and adjusted her hat. "Well, I must be going. Thank you for tea."

"And thank you for the delivery," Michael said, following her to the door. "I realize asking you not to investigate is impossible, but will you at least promise to keep me informed of what you find?"

"That I can do." She opened the door to let herself out. "Good night."

"Good night." He walked with her to the top of the stairs then placed his hand on her arm. "And feel free to stop by anytime with cake. You can even bring Dickens. I miss that cat."

"I might just do that," Hazel said as she headed downstairs. "Thank you again."

---

## CHAPTER SIX

By the time Hazel returned to Hastings Manor, dinner was served. She let Shrewsbury take her coat then headed into the dining room, inhaling the luscious smells along the way—soup, roast beef, with roasted potatoes, carrots, peas, and Yorkshire puddings with horseradish sauce and gravy, and followed by Alice's Spotted Dick pudding with custard.

"Allow me, madam," Duffy said, holding her chair for her. He helped with house duties when he wasn't driving her to and fro. With such a small staff, they all seemed to pitch in wherever they were needed. "May I get you some wine with your meal?"

"Just water tonight, I think. Thank you, Duffy." Hazel flicked open her linen napkin and stared around the room at her staff. It seemed rather silly, her eating at this big dining room table alone, but that was the way things had always been done at Hastings Manor. The staff usually ate earlier anyway, all together in the kitchen. There'd been times she'd considered joining them after her Charles passed on, but she wasn't sure their friendship extended quite that far yet, and she didn't want to overstep her bounds. "Everything looks delicious, Alice."

"Thank you, madam." The cook beamed. "I take it your trip this afternoon went well?"

"Yes, better than expected, actually." Hazel sat back slightly as Maggie set a bowl of homemade minestrone soup in front of her. She picked up her soupspoon and took a tentative sip. Warm and spicy with just a hint of sweetness from the tomatoes. "Inspector Gibson says hello and sends his thanks for the lovely cake. He thinks you're trying to fatten him up."

"That man don't need any extra bulk. He looks just fine the way he is. Such a charmer, that Inspector Gibson." Alice blushed, well and truly smitten with the chief inspector, if her pink cheeks were any indication.

Hazel's cheeks heated a bit too as she remembered him greeting her in nothing but his shirtsleeves, and how well he'd filled out said sleeves. Charles had always been more on the slim side, resembling a dashing dandy from one of the silent Hollywood films.

Whereas Michael looked more rough-and-tumble, more outdoorsy and rugged. Both were appealing, in their own ways. Alice gave her a knowing look and smile then headed back into the kitchen to bring out the next course.

Dickens sashayed into the dining room and twined around the staff's feet as the ladies and Duffy cleared away dishes. Hazel finished her soup and nibbled on a fresh-baked roll while Shrewsbury carved the beef on the sideboard. Every so often, she spied him slipping the cat small chunks of meat when he thought Hazel wasn't looking, and she couldn't help but smile. For all his mystery and bluster, the butler was as soft as butter at heart and full of contradictions. Someday she'd love to learn more about him.

Once her main course had been served and the staff were all present again, Hazel swallowed a mouthful of the melt-in-your-mouth roast beef then dabbed her mouth with her linen napkin. "I will say that after speaking with the inspector, I can conclusively say that Doris's death was definitely not a suicide."

"Really, madam?" Maggie said, her somber expression brightening. "I'm so glad you were able to convince the police of that."

"Amazing," Duffy added. "Wouldn't have thought

those coppers would do right by one of us, a mere maid."

"Actually, Michael was on the same page as I was once we discussed it. About Doris being pushed, anyway. We still have some differences as to who might be responsible. But Maggie, I swear to you that I'll do everything in my power to make sure justice is done for poor Doris."

"Well done, madam," Shrewsbury said, refilling her water glass. The trust in his eyes warmed Hazel's heart more than she could say. The fact he'd been a close confidant of her dear Charles made it all the more touching that he'd put his trust in her too. She'd always known there was a divide between the aristocracy and the servant class, but she'd never realized how much until she'd visited Farnsworth earlier. Now, she vowed to do everything in her power to make sure she kept her word to these people. Regardless of Lady Wakefield's rules about fraternizing with her staff, these people were all the family Hazel had now, and she wanted to do right by them.

"Glad to hear it, madam." Alice offered her more vegetables—a succulent mix of potatoes, carrots, and peas—which Hazel turned down, unfortunately. She'd had two servings already and felt ready to burst at the seams. "What's the first step then, on the case?" the cook asked.

"The first thing I need to do is learn as much about Doris as I can. I've got a lot of conflicting information, but from what I can tell, it's quite possible she was having an affair with Lord Wakefield or someone else in the Farnsworth household."

"Hmm." Shrewsbury frowned, his silver brows knitting. "Perhaps she was blackmailing Lord Wakefield or another member of the family."

"Or maybe she had more than one lover and they pushed her over the side of the roof in a jealous rage," Duffy said, ignoring Maggie's glare from across the room. "If she was as... err... *friendly* as people are suggesting."

"Anything is possible, I suppose." Hazel finished her last mouthful of roast beef then pushed her plate aside. "Though I've yet to figure out why she was up in that third-story room. The housekeeper said it wasn't one of Doris's duties to clean it, and it was rather gloomy and musty."

"Meeting a lover?" Duffy suggested again, drawing a growl from Maggie this time. "What?" he asked. "I'm just going with the prevailing theory."

"I'll tell you what you can do with your theory—"

Maggie balled her fists at her sides. "Doris was a good girl, I tell you. I won't have her memory besmirched."

"Besmirched?" Duffy flashed her a wide smile. "I'm delighted by your vocabulary, Mags."

"Why, I'll give you vocabulary, mister—"

"Watch yourselves," Alice interceded, giving each of the younger staff members a stern look as they cleared away the dirty dishes. "Why do you think it's Lord Wakefield, madam?"

"Because his alibi is in question, I'm afraid," Hazel said, glancing between the cook and Shrewsbury. "Detective Gibson said Lord Wakefield told the police he was at his club when the accident occurred, but then Lady Wakefield told me today that her husband was at home in his study when they heard the scream." She twined her fingers together and tapped the tips against her mouth, her gaze narrowing. "It's impossible for a man to be in two places at once."

"Very true, madam." Shrewsbury gave her a hint of a smile. "Even one as rich as Wakefield."

"So now I just need to work out who Doris might have been dallying with, where they might have been sneaking off to, and why she would have been killed over it."

Maggie returned with a generous helping of Spotted Dick and custard for Hazel. "I'm sorry, madam, but I stand by my gut and my friend. Doris was not the type to have an affair."

"How about a boyfriend then?" Hazel asked.

"I'm just not sure." Maggie compressed her lips. "Like I said, we fell out of touch for a while, but we were very close as children."

"Is there anyone else you know who might have stayed closer with Doris over the years?" Hazel took a mouthful of the stodgy sponge pudding. "Someone who might be able to fill in the missing pieces?"

"Well..." Maggie frowned. "I could ask my mum, I suppose. I could pay her a visit."

"Excellent." Hazel smiled then looked to her chauffeur, who was slouched against the wall in the corner. "I'm sure Duffy will be happy to drive you."

"Madam." The driver tipped his head to her then winked at Maggie. "Happy to drive you anywhere, Mags. In fact, if we leave now, I can drop you at your mum's then pop off to the pub and pick you up on the way back tonight."

"Oh, but I can't go now, madam." Maggie seemed a bit flustered, her cheeks flushed as she looked anywhere but at Duffy. "All this food needs to be cleared away, and—"

"Nonsense." Alice pushed the younger maid toward the door, shaking her head. "I'll clean up. We're all working on this together, remember? And while you're out, I'll pay a visit to my friend Jane too after I'm done here. Her daughter works in the kitchen over at Farnsworth Abbey. Maybe I can find something out from her too. Jane loves to gossip."

Shrewsbury cleared his throat, his posture straight as always, and his dark eyes sharp. "And I'll check that Lord Wakefield was really at his club as he claimed. I've certain connections there who can corroborate his story. People who wouldn't necessarily want to speak with the police."

"Connections?" Hazel asked the stately butler, wondering not for the first time exactly what the man's past was. She'd always suspected he might have been a secret agent or an informant or something for her husband.

She could just as easily picture him with a cloak and a dagger in a dark alleyway as she could in his pristine butler's uniform, catering to her guests and the needs of her household. His accent was a bit muddled too, part cockney, part British upper crust, and part something she couldn't quite place—Indian perhaps?

She decided to pry a bit, even though chances were slim to none she'd learn anything new about the man. His secrets seemed to be locked up tighter than the crown jewels. Yet her late husband had trusted

Shrewsbury implicitly, and that was good enough for Hazel. "What kind of connections?"

Shrewsbury smiled mysteriously and gave her a slight bow, the glow of the lights glimmering off the top of his bald head. He clicked his heels, the leather of his black boots sticking slightly. "A good butler never reveals his sources, madam."

## CHAPTER SEVEN

Hours later, Hazel finally stopped working on her book when she heard the Sunbeam pull up in front of the house. Duffy was back, which meant she needed to see what he'd discovered at the pub. She stretched and gave Dickens a good scratch behind the ears then headed downstairs to see what her staff had found through their various sources.

Reaching the first floor, she wandered into the sitting room and saw Shrewsbury and Alice already waiting for her. Duffy and Maggie soon joined them. Hazel took her regular seat in her favorite chair by the window, and Dickens soon strolled in and jumped up onto her lap.

The staff hovered near the walls, looking uncomfortable, until Hazel insisted they sit as well. They all exchanged looks before doing as she asked. Apparently, she'd crossed another of those family-staff boundaries without realizing it, but they'd just have to get used to it, because she considered them more than employees now. Besides, she'd get a crick in her neck from looking up so much.

Shrewsbury and Alice took a seat on the settee across from her, and Dickens promptly jumped down from her lap to sit between them, while Duffy and Maggie pulled up chairs on opposite ends of the settee. Hazel winced as she imagined the cat's cream-colored hair all over her mysterious butler's crisp black suit, but he never said a word, just looked supremely dignified as he stroked the feline's fur—a master of espionage and animals too. Dickens purred loudly, as if receiving the best massage of his life, and stretched out beside Shrewsbury.

"What did you all find out?" Hazel asked, biting back a laugh at her errant kitty.

"Well, madam"—Duffy removed his black driver's cap and twisted it between his hands—"I got the gossip from George Duncan, the under-butler at Farnsworth Abbey, while I was at the pub, though it's not my usual practice to talk out of turn. George said he saw Doris sneaking into the Farnsworth garage a couple of times over this past summer to slip notes to Alphonse Ash, the family's chauffeur. Then, about three weeks ago, he said, she stopped visiting the garage entirely, right after George overheard the two of them having a loud argument."

"A lover's quarrel perhaps?" Hazel asked, toeing off her shoes then slipping her feet beneath her on the chair. She'd changed from her lovely green dress into a cozy robe for the evening, but with the weather getting chillier, her feet still got cold.

"Could be," Duffy said, avoiding Maggie's pointed stare. "George suspected hanky-panky, and I'd have to say I agree. Seems the most logical reason why a maid would be visiting the garage."

"I don't know, madam," Alice said, shaking her head. "I wouldn't be too hasty there. My friend Jane told me that last Wednesday, several of the staff accompanied Lady Wakefield and the twins on a shopping trip in town. While they were there, Jane's daughter said she happened to see Doris in a cozy tête-à-tête with the Wakefields' son, Thomas, near the train station—and that wasn't the first time she'd seen the two of them meeting secretly, either."

Hazel frowned. Maybe what Mrs. Crosby suspected was true. Maybe Doris was having an affair with more than one man at a time, both Thomas and the chauffeur. From the sound of things, it seemed like a sordid love triangle straight from the pages of Peg's

Paper magazine novel. And if that scenario proved true and Doris had tried to break it off with one of her lovers, then it was possible the scorned man had decided if he couldn't have her, no one else could.

"For what it's worth, madam," Shrewsbury said, looking up from Dickens to her, his grey eyes sharp, "Lord Wakefield wasn't at his club that night."

"So he could have been home then, just as Lady Wakefield told me?"

"He could have, yes." Shrewsbury's gaze narrowed. "But why not say so to the police?"

"Odd," Maggie said. "Why wouldn't he run out like everyone else when Doris screamed?"

"Good question," Hazel said.

"Well, if you ask me"—Duffy crossed his arms, his expression thoughtful—"the lord wouldn't need to run out to see who was screaming if he was the one who pushed her."

"Pushed her?" Hazel raised a brow, frowning. "You think Lord Wakefield shoved a maid off his roof? That sounds rather drastic to me. What motive could he have?"

"Nothing's impossible, madam. History's full of instances where the aristocracy have done much, much worse," Shrewsbury added. "On a different tack, perhaps Doris was having an affair with him too, then attempted to blackmail him. That would put Wake-field in a difficult position and make him more inclined to push her."

"How ghastly!" Hazel scrunched her nose and placed her hand on her chest in horror. "An affair with a father and son both? Not to mention their chauffeur? That's beyond sordid. That's insane. How could she keep track of them all? I'm sorry, but that sounds too far-fetched."

"Agreed." Maggie scowled, her chin raised defiantly. "I told you, Doris was *not* like that. And when I talked to my mother tonight, the only thing strange she said poor Doris had done over the past month or so was talk about going on a trip. And my mum only found it strange because as far as she knew, Doris didn't have the money to travel."

"A trip?" Hazel sat forward, her instincts telling her the location might be important. "Where?"

"Mom said Doris never mentioned a specific location." Maggie shook her head. "Only that it was some place up north, because at the time Mum wondered why anyone would go there with winter approaching. The weather's bad enough here in Oxfordshire, for goodness' sake."

"Hmm." Hazel sat back. A trip to a remote location at the most inhospitable time of year. It didn't sound like her kind of romantic getaway, but perhaps if the lovebirds were desperate, any port in a storm was better than none. If she were writing one of her mysteries, the next step would be to collect alibis and follow up with the staff members she'd already spoken with at Farnsworth Abbey. The trick, though, would be returning to the Wakefields' estate without looking too suspicious. What she needed was an excuse to get back in there, something they wouldn't question, something she could use to her advantage...

"What's our next step, madam?" Alice asked, straightening her skirts and giving a snoozing Dickens beside her a side glance.

"I need to get back into the Wakefields' home." Hazel shoved her hands into the fuzzy pockets of her robe and smiled. "I'll do that tomorrow."

"Any idea how?" Duffy asked. "If they've got a killer hidden amongst them, they might close ranks and keep visitors out."

"True." Hazel cocked her head and looked over at her latest manuscript, realizing the perfect solution had been sitting before her all along. "But I have an excellent idea to get into Lady Wakefield's good graces."

## CHAPTER EIGHT

"Ah, Mrs. Martin," Lady Wakefield said, greeting Hazel in the grand hall at Farnsworth Abbey the next day. Harrison, the butler who'd let her in, bowed slightly to Hazel then disappeared into the background as Lady Wakefield brushed past him as if he weren't there. "To what do we owe the honor of a second visit?"

"I'm so sorry to show up again on your doorstep without notice, but I wanted to make sure I got the acknowledgment in my book worded exactly how you wanted it. And if it wouldn't be too much bother, I was also hoping to check one more tiny detail on the third floor for my mystery plot. The whole thing really does rely on the specifics."

At the reminder of the book's acknowledgment and inclusion of her family name, Lady Wakefield went all fluttery with anticipation, and her smile widened. "Well, certainly, Mrs. Martin. Whatever you require. Please, do go upstairs, and I'll be with you momentarily. You remember the way, don't you?"

"Yes, I remember. Thank you." Hazel followed the path Mrs. Crosby had led her on the day before and eventually ended up in the same gloomy hallway on the third floor outside the turret room. Except this time, instead of stopping at the middle door, Hazel walked straight to the end of the hall and the intriguing second door she'd seen the day before. After checking to make sure she wasn't seen, Hazel inched the door open, the metal knob cold in her palm. Wind whistled outside the walls, and dust swirled in the hazy sunshine streaming in through the window in the turret room. As the door creaked open, Hazel held her breath. She'd expected to see perhaps a second set of stairs or another form of escape route for Doris's murderer. What she found behind the door, however, was an attic—a sealed attic at that, with no other exit— which meant whoever pushed Doris wouldn't have been able to run down a back staircase to avoid being seen.

*Darn it!*

Hazel had just started to peer around the dim space cluttered with old furniture, steamer trunks, piles of clothing and furs bunched in a corner, as well as other remnants of the past, when footsteps sounded on the stairs behind her, and her heartbeat quickened. Time to go. Hazel hurried to close the attic door and rushed down the hall to the turret room, doing her best to look as if she were inspecting the tiny space. Lady Wakefield appeared moments later, her placid expression from the grand hall now harried and upset.

"I just don't understand about this murder business. I thought this would all be over and done with by now and we could move on from such tragedy," she said, clasping the long string of pearls around her neck and twining them around her fingers. The pale peach of her day dress only served to wash out her already pallid complexion and made her dark eyes look nearly black. "Detective Chief Inspector Gibson was here earlier too. He informed us the police were now considering Doris's death to be murder." She shook her head, her voice dropping to little more than a scandalized whisper. "A murder. Can you imagine? I shudder to think what the other families are saying about us behind our backs. It's all got me so unsettled. I've no idea why the police are putting so much effort into the death of a little tart."

"I'm sorry," Hazel said, doing her best to hide her shock and growing anger from her tone. Yes, she'd considered the possibility that poor Doris had been involved in some type of illicit affair, but none of that had been confirmed as of yet, and it certainly didn't make her a tart.

What left Hazel most unsettled was the fact Lady Wakefield had lost a member of her household staff and could remain so callous about it, worrying more about her reputation than justice for the victim. Still, she couldn't afford to alienate this woman or her family until she got to the bottom of Doris's death. So she played along with the woman's distress as best she could.

Hazel forced her most conciliatory smile and patted Lady Wakefield's arm. "It's a terrible thing you're dealing with, I'm sure. Did the inspector say what changed their minds, or have you heard any rumors as to why the police might suspect foul play?"

"No, not really." Lady Wakefield sighed and turned her back on the turret room. "Though Mrs. Crosby did mention Doris might have been despondent over a lover. I certainly can't imagine why else anyone would choose to come up to this dingy place unless it was for a romantic tryst, but then I'm not a servant either. Maybe conducting an illicit affair under our noses gave her some kind of cheap thrill."

Hazel didn't miss the sharp edge to the woman's

tone or the narrowing of her dark eyes as she'd said the last words. They headed back downstairs again, passing a small sitting room where the Wakefield twins sat beside a fire, heads together as if deep in conversation. Lady Wakefield stopped just outside the door and motioned for Hazel to keep quiet by holding her index finger to her lips.

Thomas had his arm around Eugenia, who still looked pale and shaken, her hands clenched tight in her lap. Her white-blond hair was held back by a sky-blue ribbon that matched the shade of her day dress. Thomas was wearing a shirt in a deeper shade of blue to match his eyes, and black trousers and braces. His red hair was several shades lighter than his mother's auburn. He looked up and caught the ladies watching them then kissed his sister's temple and murmured, "It will all work out, sis. Don't worry."

"I'm so worried about my daughter," Lady Wakefield whispered to Hazel, breaking her concentration. "Eugenia's taken this accident so hard. I just hope it won't affect her marital prospects." Then she smiled and spoke loudly as she led Hazel into the room. "Ah, here are the twins. Have I told you how proud I am to be arranging an engagement between my Thomas and the Tewkesbury girl? She comes from such good breeding and old money."

Thomas looked up from his sister, giving a curt nod to Hazel before glaring at his mother. "In case you've forgotten, it's 1923, and I prefer to pick my own girls."

"Oh, pshaw." Lady Wakefield gave a dismissive wave in her son's direction. "We have the family name to think about, and the legacy of the Farnsworth estate to deal with. You're heir to a title, Thomas, and as such, you have responsibilities. You're the only son. You carry the family name onwards to the next generation. Tomorrow, we attend breakfast with the Tewkesburys, and I expect you to be *receptive* to their offer and their daughter."

At the mention of her brother's impending engagement, Eugenia burst into a fresh round of tears, and Lady Wakefield rushed to her side to comfort her. "There, there, dear. I think perhaps you should not attend, Eugenia. Even though it might be good for you to get out a bit, in your state, it might only make things worse." She laid a hand across her daughter's forehead and sighed. "I don't like your color, far too pale. And you've lost weight too, I can tell. You haven't been eating nearly enough lately."

Eugenia only sobbed harder.

"Oh no. Please don't cry so, dear." Lady Wakefield

pulled the crying girl's stiff form into her side, seemingly unaware of her daughter's obvious discomfort and her son's heated glare. Instead, she glanced up at Hazel and gave her a tight smile. "I'm so sorry you must be party to such unseemly hysterics, Mrs. Martin. But as I said, she and Doris were so close." She went to stroke Eugenia's hair, but the girl pulled away. "Now, with all the upset, my daughter has stopped eating. She's barely touched her breakfast for the past several days, which isn't like her at all. Too bad, really, since she'll need all her strength to catch an earl this season."

Hazel watched the uncomfortable scene, the animosity between children and parent clear as day. What she really needed to do next was get Eugenia alone so she could question her—Thomas too, if possible. But with Lady Wakefield hovering around like a concerned, overprotective hen, sequestering the twins alone anytime soon didn't seem likely. At least she'd accomplished her goal for the day—seeing what was behind that second door on the third floor.

Backing toward the sitting room door, Hazel sighed. "I should really be going now. Need to get that writing time in. I can see myself out. Thank you again for your hospitality and indulging my author's whims to investigate the turret room once more, Lady Wakefield. We can discuss the acknowledgement at a more convenient time."

Without waiting for a response, Hazel headed out into the hallway, creeping toward the family wing, where Lord Wakefield's study was located. Once she reached the end of the hall and made a left, she spotted Lady Wakefield's sewing room again. A quick peek inside showed that yes, there was a mirror above the sewing machine, just as Lady Wakefield had said, and it was positioned perfectly to spy on her husband across the hall. Still, the niggling suspicion that Lady Wakefield might have been covering for her errant husband the night of Doris's death refused to abate. Was it possible, as Shrewsbury and Duffy suspected, that Lord Wakefield could've been having an affair with poor Doris and that jealousy might have had something to do with the murder?

After a look both ways to make sure she wasn't observed, Hazel tiptoed across the hall to look inside Lord Wakefield's study. Inside, she found Norwich watching her, his black fur gleaming in the glow of the fire, his green eyes knowing. Her gaze skimmed the dark mahogany desk and tufted leather chairs, lighting on the velvet-draped French doors. It would be easy to slip outside without his wife noticing. If he had been the one to push Doris that night, it seemed impossible

that he could have done so and not been seen by someone, given the distance between this wing of the house
and the third-floor stairs. Making a mental note of it
all, Hazel turned to leave, only to be halted by a
quiet "Psst."

Startled, Hazel glanced to her left to see one of the
housemaids poking her head out of the room at the end
of the hall. She waved Hazel over to what turned out
to be the library and pulled her into the shadows of the
room, where she whispered, "I'm Betsy, madam. The
word around the town is that you're looking after what
happened to Doris."

Hazel nodded.

"I've heard about you. They say you're a friend of
the workers and your staff says you're fair and trustworthy and all..."

"I'm flattered they think so." Hazel warmed at the
thought that her staff talked about her in those compli-
mentary terms. She flashed what she hoped was a
friendly smile toward the nervous maid. "Is there
something you want to tell me?"

"Yes, madam." Betsy wrung her hands. "I over-
heard Doris arguing in Lord Wakefield's study last
Thursday, madam. One week exactly before she died.
I couldn't hear all of what they were fighting about, nor

could I identify the other person's voice, but I did hear Doris yelling about not being paid off."

"Paid off?" Hazel frowned. "Someone was trying to pay her off? For what?"

"I'm not entirely sure, madam. Believe me, madam, I wasn't trying to eavesdrop, honestly. I just couldn't help overhearing, like I said. Down here on the first floor, this wing is very quiet, you see, with only the lord's study and the lady's sewing room and then this library at the end." Betsy shrugged, not meeting Hazel's gaze. "No one visits much during the day as there's no way of passing through. You have to go back out into the main part of the house to get anywhere else."

"And this is normally your section of the house to clean?" Hazel asked, wondering what else Betsy might have seen during the course of her duties.

"Yes, madam." Betsy sniffed. "It's my job to dust the spines of the books in the library every Thursday night, and that was what I was doing when the argument happened. That's what I was doing two nights ago when poor Doris died too."

"Oh, well then, I was wondering if you might remember—"

"Betsy? We need you in the sitting room, please,"

Lady Wakefield called from the end of the hall. "Now, Betsy."

The maid tensed then gave Hazel a look. "Sorry, madam. I need to go. Wait here a few minutes while I attend to the family and keep them occupied, then head to the big hall. Harrison will let you out, no questions asked. Do you remember the way, madam?"

Hazel nodded then watched as the maid disappeared, leaving her alone in the library. Amidst the smell of old books and furniture polish, she waited as requested until the coast was clear and all was quiet again before winding her way back to the grand hall. Harrison greeted her with another bow and a small smile as he let her out of the house. Having friends in the staff most definitely had its rewards.

---

## CHAPTER NINE

**B**ack at Hastings Manor later that morning, Hazel settled in to work on her book again, her jade Radite Sheaffer pen in hand and toast and tea from Alice on the desk beside her. The sunlight streaming in through the windows warmed her skin, and she pulled her cream-colored shawl tighter around her shoulders.

Dickens meowed from the other side of the desk, playing with the end of her pen as she attempted to write. In this new scene she was drafting today, her detective hero, Archibald Fox, was trying to work out which one of his suspects was lying. The irony was not lost on her, as Hazel tried to discover the same thing about the Wakefield family. One of them had to be making up their alibi. One always did.

After thirty minutes of not putting one single word

on paper, however, Hazel put down her pen and picked up her toast instead, nibbling on the buttery snack, musing to Dickens about her case while he lay there, adorably swiping his paws over his face then licking them.

"Maggie's mum said Doris was going on a trip up north, but why would she? Winter's coming, and most ladies' maids don't just up and go on trips alone anyway. Was she running away or being sent away?"

Dickens stopped and stared at her, meowing loudly before resuming his grooming.

"And where was Lord Wakefield when Doris fell, hmm?" She swallowed another mouthful of toast then brushed the crumbs from the front of her navy wool dress. "If he was in his study, then why didn't he come running out like everyone else? Shrewsbury confirmed he wasn't at his club as he'd originally claimed, so if he wasn't there and he wasn't in his study, then where exactly was he?"

The cat took a sudden interest in a shiny paperclip on her desk, batting it around like a ball then attacking it as if it were a fierce opponent.

"And was Doris truly as loose as Lady Wakefield and Mrs. Crosby have suggested? Fooling around with the chauffeur and passing notes to him while also dallying with both Thomas and his father?" She popped the last piece of the toast in her mouth then picked up her tea, sipping the luke-warm, milky liquid. "And where was this missing chauffeur when Doris fell, hmm? Mrs. Crosby claimed he was down in the garage, which would make sense, I suppose, but she couldn't really confirm his location for sure, could she? No, because she was in the house at the time. Maybe I need to look into that."

Sighing, Hazel sat back and sipped her tea while Dickens batted the paperclip off the desk and onto the floor then moved back to batting her pen with his paw, rolling onto his back with the pen clasped tight between his paws like a baton. "Then there's the whole convoluted matter of timing. If someone pushed Doris, would they have time to run back down the stairs before the others came up to investigate her screams? I did find the attic today and suppose the killer could've hidden in there, but that would mean they'd be trapped inside that stuffy space until everyone else had left the turret room. I suppose they could have waited for those who ran up to run back down again, and then sneaked out and joined them. Very risky, I say. And they wouldn't stay in there since their absence would be noticed, and I'd think the police would look behind that door too during their investigation. I'll make a note to ask Michael about that, because if they didn't, then that might explain where Lord Wakefield was. Still, I can't picture him hiding in there the whole time." She exhaled, her shoulders slumping. "And if the killer wasn't hiding in the attic, it must have been someone who either wasn't in the turret room or wasn't seen on the ground."

Dickens meowed again as the pen fell from his paws and clattered onto the desk. Hazel looked up and narrowed her gaze on him. "And who exactly was Doris arguing with in the lord's study that night? Logic says it was Lord Wakefield, or perhaps Thomas, given it was in the family's private wing. And what exactly were they fighting about? Was she blackmailing Lord Wakefield for money to go on this trip of hers, as Shrewsbury suggested? And if that's the case, then what's the chauffeur got to do with it all?"

Hazel sat forward at last and grabbed Dickens's paw before he dunked it in her teacup. "Eugenia knows something, doesn't she, boy?" She laughed, shaking his foot like a tiny hand. "Yes, I agree, she does. I say we pay her a visit tomorrow morning after Lady Wakefield and Thomas leave for that ghastly breakfast at the Tewkesburys', eh?"

THAT NIGHT, Hazel just couldn't face eating another meal alone at the big dining room table. It reminded her too much of the dinners she'd shared with her Charles, even with all the staff around. So, instead, she sneaked downstairs early and tiptoed around to the kitchen door in her stockinged feet. There, she peeked in at her staff enjoying their nightly meal together, minus Shrewsbury. She hadn't dined with the staff since she'd been a child, but there was such comfort surrounding her household employees now that Hazel was nearly desperate for their company. Besides, being fussed over and served wasn't her favorite thing.

Hazel cleared her throat to alert them to her presence. "May I join you in here tonight for dinner?"

The staff looked up and exchanged looks, then Alice waved her over, her smile warm as she gestured to an empty seat near the end of the table. "Please do, madam."

"Thanks." She took her place then helped herself to leftover roast beef and vegetables from the night before as they were passed to her. In addition, there were fresh mashed potatoes, yummy roasted chicken, green beans from the kitchen garden—all her favorite hearty, tasty comfort food. She devoured a plateful then went back for seconds, finally settling back in her seat, full and content and amongst friends. It was one of the few times she'd felt this way since Charles had died. "I went to the Wakefields' again this morning to check out a few things."

"What did you find, madam?" Duffy asked, knife and fork in hand. "If you don't mind me asking."

"Well, one of the housemaids, Betsy, said she'd overheard Doris arguing with someone in Lord Wakefield's study a week before she died."

"Wonder what that's about?" Alice said, wiping her mouth. "Arguing with the master is never a good thing."

"I'm not sure yet," Hazel said, pouring herself a glass of water. "The only words Betsy heard clearly from Doris were 'not paid off.'" Unfortunately, I haven't yet worked out what they mean or how they're related to her death."

"Hmm." Duffy looked thoughtful. "That seems to imply blackmail. Perhaps she had information about Lord Wakefield he didn't want her telling anyone. Which goes back to what Shrewsbury said."

"Yes, that's what I thought—" Hazel started, only to be interrupted by the stately butler himself entering and giving her a slight bow in his official uniform.

"Inspector Gibson is here, madam."

Before Hazel could tell Shrewsbury to show the

chief inspector into the sitting room, he appeared beside the butler in the kitchen doorway.

"Inspector Gibson," Hazel said, wiping her mouth with her napkin and feeling decidedly off-kilter at being seen so informally. "I wasn't expecting you tonight."

"Oh, that's my fault, madam," Alice said, gesturing for Duffy and Maggie to scoot down a place to make room for the new arrival. "I invited him over to have a glass of beer with the men and must have forgotten to mention it to you."

As the inspector took a seat across the table from Hazel, Alice sliced him off a huge piece of apple pie and slid it in front of him. Michael smiled and thanked the cook, giving Hazel a warm, slightly embarrassed smile. "I certainly hope I'm not intruding."

"No, no." Hazel gave Alice a look, not missing her cat-ate-the-canary grin and picked up her fork once more. "Not at all, Inspector Gibson. We were all just discussing Doris's case. Your timing is perfect, actually."

"Glad to hear it." He dug into his pie with gusto. For a man who ate so much, he certainly kept himself in excellent shape. "So, give me an update on your investigation. What have you found? Anything new today?"

"Well, as I was just telling the staff a moment ago, I went back to Farnsworth Abbey this morning to double-check a few things, and one of the maids pulled me aside. Betsy said that a week before the accident, she overheard Doris arguing with someone in Lord Wakefield's study."

"Really? What exactly did she hear? Who was talking?"

He seemed genuinely interested in her information and opinions, something Hazel hadn't felt since Charles was alive. Still, she wasn't sure how much to share with him at this point. After all, she wasn't an official member of the police force. She thanked Alice for the piece of pie the cook placed in front of her, then refocused on the Inspector. "Unfortunately, the maid couldn't identify the other party's voice in the fight, but she did say she distinctly heard Doris say the words 'not paid off.'"

"Interesting." Gibson devoured half his slice of pie in two mouthfuls before continuing. "Meaning she hadn't been paid off, or she wouldn't be paid off? The answer could turn things in a whole different direction." He shook his head. "Well, our investigation found something new today too. Lord Wakefield was not at his club the night of Doris's death as he'd claimed."

"Oh my," Hazel said, feigning her best surprised tone. She already knew that, of course, thanks to Shrewsbury and his infinite mysterious contacts. She glanced over at the butler, who stood near the wall, his stoic expression intact. "That puts him squarely in the suspect column then, I suppose."

"It does." Michael smiled, the warmth reaching his eyes. "What else did you find?"

"My maid, Maggie, heard through the grapevine that Doris was planning a trip north. And Alice has a friend whose daughter works in the kitchens at Farnsworth and said Thomas Wakefield was seen in a tête-à-tête with Doris last week on an errand in town." Hazel nibbled on the rich, sweet filling of her apple pie, savoring the shortcrust pastry on top. "Seems strange a person would plan to travel up to the northern regions with winter coming on, doesn't it?"

"Hmm. It does. Unless that person didn't want to be found, or bothered." Michael sat back as Alice slid another slice of pie onto his plate. "The best cook in all the land. Thank you, Alice."

The older woman blushed as she returned to the sink to wash the dinner dishes.

"Funny you should mention Thomas," Michael said, digging into his second slice. "There's been some gossip about an argument between him and the Wake-fields' chauffeur, Alphonse Ash."

"Really?" Hazel filed that new information away for later. "Perhaps they were arguing over Doris. Word has it she used to sneak out to pass notes to Alphonse in the garage, but that stopped after they fought a few weeks ago."

"None of that, however, explains why Lord Wake-field lied about his whereabouts the night of Doris's death." Gibson finished his last mouthful of pie then sat back, patting his trim, flat stomach. Hazel had always admired Charles's sky-high metabolism. It seemed men could eat whatever they wanted and stay slim, while she had to watch every little mouthful, or she'd quickly outgrow her new wardrobe.

The inspector shook his head. "If he's not the killer, he's got nothing to hide, right?"

Hazel tilted her head, her gaze narrowed. "Yes, but what if he is the killer? Then the question becomes what did Thomas and Alphonse have to do with things?"

"Good point." He leaned forward and rested his forearms on the table as the other servants got up to finish clearing the table. "And where exactly was Doris going on her trip? The north country is pretty broad. And where did she get the money? Is that what she meant by 'not paid off'? Had Doris not yet received passage for her trip?"

"I'm just not sure about any of it at this point." Hazel sighed then sipped her tea. "That doesn't make any sense. If someone was paying her off, then why go to the trouble of killing her?"

"Unless more than one person wanted to keep her quiet." Michael pushed to his feet and grabbed his hat from the sideboard where he'd laid it when he came in. "All things to consider. I have to say, though, the thing that still bothers me is how did the killer lure her to that obscure turret room?"

"That is a mystery." Hazel rose as well to escort her guest back toward the front door. They walked out into the dining room side by side. "Maybe that was the spot where she always met this person, like a lover. Or maybe they lured her there by saying they were going to deliver the money for the payoff."

"If that's the case, then that signifies intent." In the hall, Gibson slipped his hat back on over his thick dark-brown curls, his voice turning serious.

"Indeed. And I suppose the police searched that attic room down the hall from the turret room." Hazel tried to keep her tone nonchalant. The last thing she wanted was for Michael to think she was trying to tell him how to do his job.

"Naturally." Michael's eyes twinkled with amusement, then he turned serious. "Listen, I appreciate all the legwork you've done to this point, but murder is serious business, and I don't want to see you get hurt."

Both touched and annoyed by his concern, she squared her shoulders and raised her chin. "Thank you for the warning, Inspector Gibson, but I assure you that I am a big girl and can decide for myself about the risks and dangers of involvement in this case."

She was about to say more, but Shrewsbury appeared around the corner with the inspector's jacket. The sly butler disappeared again just as quickly, leaving Hazel to deal with the awkward moment.

"Well, then," Michael said, giving her a small smile.

"Yes." Hazel placed her hand on the knob, feeling as if she should say something more but not knowing what. "Thank you for stopping by, Inspector Gibson."

"Michael," he said then studied her for a few seconds. "May I ask you something?"

Her pulse quickened. In a previous moment, very similar to this one, during the Myrtle Pembroke case, he'd asked Hazel to dinner. She liked him, a lot, but she still wasn't ready for that sort of thing. Was she? Of course not. She'd say no, definitely. Well, maybe one

dinner wouldn't be such a bad thing. She *should* cultivate him as a friend, because he did come in handy
with these investigations and he was not hard on
the eyes.

"Yes..." She drew the word out, wondering where
he might take her. Perhaps that new French
restaurant...

"Will you tell Alice her pie was divine?" Michael
reached into his pocket and pulled out a card. "Ring
me if you find out anything that can help catch the
killer."

And with that, he opened the door, nodded a goodbye, and left.

_____

## CHAPTER TEN

Hazel was back at Farnsworth Abbey the next day, this time lurking outside near the Sunbeam, where Duffy waited behind the wheel. They'd parked off to the side of the grand manor this time, behind a copse of trees, to wait for Lady Wakefield and Thomas to leave so she could get inside to question Eugenia.

The sun was shining, but the air was still brisk this early in the day, so she'd once again donned her new brocade coat—this time over a deep-plum charmeuse long-sleeved day dress with silver buttons up the front and a matching brimmed hat.

She hid near Duffy's door on the driver's side of the car, ignoring her chauffeur's amused glances as she tried to duck and cover once Lady Wakefield and Thomas emerged from the house and approached their sleek grey Daimler limousine. From his sullen expression, Thomas wasn't any more excited about breakfast with the Tewkesburys than he'd been the day before.

Once the pair had departed, Hazel smoothed her hand down the front of her dress and straightened her hat, checking her appearance in the vehicle's side mirror, before approaching Farnsworth Abbey and knocking on the front door. Feeling an odd thrill of nerves, she patted the back of her hair, hoping her jaunt at hiding hadn't mussed it up too badly.

Harrison, the butler, answered on her second knock, looking as prim as usual. "Good day, madam. May I help you?"

"Yes, I'm here to see Miss Eugenia Wakefield, please." Hazel gave him a bright smile, hoping he wouldn't boot her right back down the front steps. Surprisingly, he smiled back.

"Certainly, madam." He gestured her into the hall then closed the heavy oak door behind her, his black uniform and white shirt crisp enough to cut someone. "This way, madam."

If Harrison thought anything strange about Hazel showing up unannounced right after the mistress of the abbey and her son had departed, he didn't show it. Then again, she suspected the staff at Farnsworth weren't so different from her own back at Hastings

Manor—tight-knit and in constant communication about the goings-on of their employers. Given that they'd most certainly been gossiping about poor Doris's demise and Hazel's earlier visits, it was entirely possible Betsy had mentioned her conversation with Hazel the previous day, as well as the discussions she'd had with Mrs. Crosby.

The stately older gentleman showed Hazel into a brightly lit breakfast room, where Eugenia sat alone at a large round table. Before her was an assortment of silver-domed dishes and fresh fruits. All the poor girl had on her plate, however, was a piece of dry toast. She looked even paler and gaunter than she had the day before, if that were possible, and dark circles shadowed the delicate skin beneath her eyes, as if she hadn't slept well in a very long time.

Hazel remembered that Lady Wakefield had mentioned her daughter's lack of appetite since the accident the day before, and that looked to still be the case. Not that the poor thing could afford to lose weight—she was painfully thin as it was. Eugenia had always been slim by nature, from what Hazel remembered, but this was unhealthy. Even her normally creamy complexion had gone slightly grey. Her blonde hair was flat and dull, and her pale-blue eyes had taken on a haunted look, only accentuated by the way her gaze constantly darted around, as if she were expecting a monster to emerge from every corner. She started a bit as Harrison strode into the room.

A wave of sympathy for the girl washed over Hazel, and she forced a smile and stepped into the room behind the butler. Whatever was wrong with the poor thing, she looked as though she could use a good friend to talk to. "Good morning, Eugenia. I do hope you don't mind me stopping by unexpectedly this morning."

"Mrs. Martin," Eugenia said, looking up at her with a surprised expression, as if just then realizing she and Harrison weren't alone. Her gaze quickly dropped back to her lap, and the corners of her mouth turned downward. "I'm afraid my mother is out."

"Oh no," Hazel said, her tone brimming with fake disappointment. "And I was hoping to speak with her about that acknowledgement today too." She slipped off her coat and handed it to the butler then took a seat beside Eugenia at the table. The girl's pink cotton dress did nothing to help her appearance. It looked wrinkled and mussed, as if Eugenia might have napped in it, or cried long and hard in it. "Well, as long as I'm here, why don't we have a chat? I was so sorry to hear about what happened to poor Doris. I do hope you're doing all right after all that nastiness. It must have been such a shock to lose a good friend like Doris, especially so close to her trip."

"Trip?" Eugenia asked, her teacup trembling in her delicate hand. "What trip?"

Hazel frowned. "Oh, perhaps I was mistaken. I could have sworn my maid, Maggie, had mentioned Doris traveling in the near future, maybe up north. Didn't you know about that?"

"No. I didn't."

"Right." Hazel helped herself to a cup of tea and took a piece of toast from beneath one of the covered dishes, pulling another one out for Eugenia as well in hopes she might get her to eat a little something. "Well, anyway. Sounds like your brother was close to Doris as well. Nearly as close with her as the two of you are, eh?"

Eugenia gave her a sideways glance, frowning. "Not really. No. Doris was my maid, so I can't imagine why she'd have much to do with my brother."

"True enough." She slathered on butter and some homemade raspberry jam onto her toast then took a bite of the sweet, savory goodness, not missing the fact Eugenia's still sat untouched on her plate. There was definitely something amiss with the girl, that much of what Lady Wakefield said was true. Hazel was determined to work out what that was, one way or another, and continued her line of questioning about the murder. "It makes one wonder, though, doesn't it? What a young woman like Doris would have to be involved with to get herself killed like that."

For the first time since Hazel had entered the breakfast room, bright-red color infused Eugenia's cheeks. She looked Hazel directly in the eye, her gaze now sparkling with anger. "Doris was not 'involved' with anything. She was a nice person, a person whom one could count on. A person who stood up for what she believed in." The amount of passion in the girl's tone had Hazel seriously rethinking her assumptions about Doris being a blackmailer and a loose woman. Perhaps Mrs. Crosby had been wrong. Maggie certainly thought Doris was a paragon of virtue. Now, apparently, so did Eugenia.

Maybe poor Doris had just been in the wrong place at the wrong time.

"My apologies," Hazel said, hoping to smooth Eugenia's ruffled feathers and get the conversation back on track. "I didn't mean to upset you, my dear. It's just all so strange. And if we're this unsettled about Doris's death, I can't imagine what the household staff is going through. I know even my employees at Hastings Manor are distraught over the loss. I'd imagine here at Farnsworth it's affected everyone, especially the maids who were her friends, and even the chauffeur. I heard Doris was especially close with him."

Eugenia gripped the edge of the table so tightly Hazel feared the wood would crack, and swallowed hard. "I wouldn't know," she whispered. "But I imagine they'd be upset."

"And to see the body like that after she fell." Hazel gave an exaggerated shudder. "Did you have to witness it too, Eugenia?"

"No." What little color that had blossomed in her cheeks disappeared, leaving the tense girl looking even more ghostlike than before. She blinked several times as if centering herself. "I was...*indisposed* when Doris screamed. By the time I came out of my room, everyone was already outside. Then Mary, the housemaid, rushed in crying and told me what had happened. She told me not to look." She squeezed her eyes shut. "That's how I found out."

Hazel leaned forward slightly with interest. "Not from your mother or father or brother?"

"No. It was Mary that told me about Doris."

"I'm so sorry." Sitting back, Hazel clasped her hands in her lap. "Where were they?"

"My family?" Eugenia glanced at her, that guarded look back in her eyes. "I'm not sure. Contacting the police and calming the servants, I suppose."

"Right." Hazel finished her tea then stood, hailing the butler for her coat. "Well, then. I'll leave you in peace, Eugenia. Again, I'm so sorry for your loss. I'll call again another time to speak with your mother about the acknowledgement. Thank you, dear."

Eugenia merely nodded, her gaze locked on the floral centerpiece on the table.

Hazel followed Harrison back out into the hall and slipped her arms back into her coat while he held it for her. When she turned back around, she nearly tripped over their cat, Norwich, who must've snuck up behind her as she'd left the sitting room. Despite the butler's rather sour look at the animal, Hazel bent to pet the cat, smiling as the feline swished his tail and stared at her with unblinking pale-green eyes, his lush black fur gleaming in the sunlight streaming through the nearby windows. "If only you could talk, Norwich. I bet you know all the secrets about this place, don't you?"

"Ah, Mrs. Martin," Mrs. Crosby said, bustling into the hall and taking Hazel by the arm to pull her aside, out of earshot of the butler. "I just wanted to ask if you could please be careful what you say to poor Miss Eugenia. She's very delicate right now, and she trusted Doris. I just don't want to see her get hurt."

Stunned, Hazel blinked. "Whatever do you mean?"

Mrs. Crosby wrung her hands, her expression worried. "It's just that Doris wasn't always doing right by Eugenia."

"Oh?"

"Doris used to run errands for her mistress, but she might have abused her trust. Last week we were sent to Bond Street together. Lady Wakefield wanted me to get her furs out of storage for the winter season, and Doris needed to pick something up at the chemist. Afterward, we were to meet up at the milliner's. But I got done a bit early, and that's when I saw Doris not at the chemist as she was supposed to be, but at Lady Etienne's." The woman leaned closer, her tone scandalous. "You know, the *delicates* shop?"

Hazel leaned back, frowning. "Perhaps she was getting something for Eugenia."

"Pardon me for saying, but of course not, madam." The older woman blanched. "Miss Eugenia's a good girl. She'd never wear the sorts of things they sell in that establishment."

As someone who'd never been quite brave enough to enter Lady Etienne's, even when her Charles had been alive, Hazel had to admire Doris's spirit. "Maybe she wanted to purchase something for herself then. It is 1923, and what was once considered taboo is now becoming more acceptable. Why, just look at our fashions." She turned a visible ankle for Mrs. Crosby to see as an example.

"Be that as it may, madam, Doris should've saved such errands for her own time, not during working hours." Mrs. Crosby frowned, seemingly ignoring Hazel's interested stare. "But Doris was just that type, wasn't she? Always bold as brass. Anyway, later, when I asked Doris about where she'd been, she said just at the chemist's. Lied right to my face. I'm guessing whatever it was she bought in that place, she was hiding it, and for good reason too. Even if those lacy clothes weren't sinful, there's no way Doris would be able to afford them on her maid's salary alone."

BACK OUTSIDE FARNSWORTH ABBEY, Hazel rushed through the door Duffy held open for her then waited until he was settled behind the wheel again. "Please take me to Bond Street. Pronto!"

Lady Etienne's was notorious for their risqué lingerie—perfect for wearing beneath those skimpy, sheath-style flapper dresses that Hazel was just now getting used to. But today, the lacy nothings beneath would have to wait. She was on a mission.

And Mrs. Crosby still seemed adamant about Doris and her wayward character too. If what she'd told her about Doris was true, then it was quite possible she was buying something to wear for one of her lovers. By talking to the assistants at the shop, she hoped to find out exactly what Doris had bought that day and who paid for the purchases.

Duffy pulled up in front of the quaint-looking French shop twenty minutes later, and Hazel went inside while her driver waited at the curb. A petite woman, about Hazel's age, approached almost immediately.

"Bonjour. Welcome to Lady Etienne's," the assistant said, her words heavily accented. In contrast to the luxury surrounding them, the tiny French lady was dressed in a plain brown cotton dress, her hair pinned back into a tight bun, and a tape measure slung around her neck. "How may I assist you today?"

"Oh, I'm not here for myself." Hazel eyed a see-through lace negligee with trepidation, heat rising in her cheeks despite her earlier bravado about being a modern woman. Deep inside, she still saw herself as a dowdy housewife who'd neglected her appearance for far too long. "I was hoping to find out some information about a purchase made by a friend of mine."

The woman gave her a suspicious look. "Are you with the police?"

"No, no. Strictly asking for myself."

"Hmm." The assistant harrumphed. "We are very busy. I cannot guarantee I will remember. What does your friend look like?"

"Well, let me see." Hazel described Doris as best she could. She'd only been to Farnsworth a handful of times and wasn't sure even which maid was Doris. Luckily, she had a good memory and a keen mind for detail. It helped with her writing and came in handy in investigations as well. She reached back in her memory, picturing all the maids she'd seen on her trips to Farnsworth Abbey, and took a guess, knowing that Doris wasn't any of the maids she'd seen on recent visits. "She was about my height, dark-blond hair that she usually wore back in a chignon. Medium build, late twenties. Brown eyes. She might have been wearing a maids' uniform when she came in."

The woman seemed to consider this a moment, her gaze narrowed and her hands on her hips. "Yes, I do remember her. It was an unusual purchase, and she seemed very nervous that someone would see her."

"Yes, that sounds like Doris." Hazel gave the woman what she hoped was a confident smile. "Do you have a receipt I could look at?"

"Perhaps." The woman walked behind the large wooden counter at the back of the store and rifled through a box of papers until she pulled one out and handed it to Hazel.

She stared down at the receipt, not spotting anything out of the ordinary, just the customary numbers and totals. "What was so unusual about the purchase?"

"The woman was very slim and tiny, not an ounce of fat on her. But she bought a pregnancy corset, the new kind that flatters the flapper styles and binds you tightly, to keep you looking slimmer longer." The woman crossed her arms, her frown deepening. "What made it so strange, though, was her demeanor. Most women who buy these corsets still can't wait to crow about their pregnancies, but this one was very secretive about hers. In fact, she was in such a hurry to leave, she didn't even take her copy of the receipt."

Hazel left the shop even more perplexed than before. If she connected the dots and Doris had been pregnant, then that added a whole new dimension to the case, and a whole new set of reasons why one of her lovers might have wanted Doris to disappear.

## CHAPTER ELEVEN

"She was what?" Maggie asked, eyes wide as saucers as she stirred a bowl of cake-mix.

Hazel had summoned her three house staff members to the kitchen upon returning. Duffy had already got an earful during the journey back to Hastings Manor and had retreated to the garage to work on the Resta, he said, though Hazel suspected he just wanted some quiet time alone.

"I'm afraid to say that all my evidence so far is pointing to your friend Doris being pregnant," Hazel said as gently as possible, knowing it would come as a shock to Maggie, the most ardent defender of Doris's reputation.

"I just don't believe it." Maggie shook her head, the shock evident in her shaky voice and trembling hands as she plopped down into an empty seat at the table. "I mean it's happened to a few other girls I know, but I never thought Doris would be like them..."

Alice stood near the door, having a standoff with Dickens. Broom in hand, she watched as the cat toyed with her by sticking one paw over the threshold. As soon as she'd start to move, however, Dickens would sit back on his haunches and groom himself leisurely as if he'd done nothing wrong.

Hazel bit back a smile. Clever boy.

Shrewsbury sighed emphatically and scowled. "Well, this certainly adds a new level of complexity. Did someone not want the baby discovered? Could that be why Doris was killed? Surely the police must be adding potential lovers to the suspect pool."

"Surely." Hazel wondered why Michael hadn't mentioned the pregnancy. She was certain there had been an autopsy. Perhaps he felt uncomfortable talking about such a delicate subject with her. Thoughts of broaching the subject with him made her a little uncomfortable too.

"But who would want to harm an unborn baby?" Alice said, furious, swatting at the cat with the broom once more. "It's unconscionable."

"Yes, I agree." Hazel leaned her elbow on the table and rested her chin in her hand, trying to wrap her head around all the new information she'd gathered

that morning. "Though the pregnancy would definitely cause an issue if the father was Lord Wakefield
or Thomas. I can't imagine the scandal something like
that would cause for such an old and aristocratic
family."

"And you think they solved the issue by killing
Doris and the baby?" Maggie asked.

"I just don't know." Hazel tapped her fingers
against her cheek as she spoke, a habit she'd developed
to bring her thoughts into focus when she was plotting
a new book. "Then again, maybe the killer wasn't the
father. Maybe it was someone else who was jealous of
Doris for having another man's baby. That brings us
back to the spurned-lover theory. And Inspector
Gibson did say Thomas and Alphonse were rumored
to have argued."

"Wait." Alice joined them at the table after giving
Dickens a final warning look. "You said last night that
Doris was going on a trip. Maybe she had both
Thomas and the chauffeur as lovers and was going
away with the one who fathered the baby. And maybe
the other one didn't like that idea and offed
poor Doris."

"Two of the girls I knew who got in trouble like
that had to go away because they didn't want anyone
to know." Maggie sighed, her shoulders slumped and

the bowl of cake-mix resting in her lap. "Poor, poor Doris."

"Back when I was young, a girl would have to go away to her sister's or another relative's so no one would discover her...*situation.*" Alice took the seat beside Hazel's. "Couple of times, those married sisters or relatives then took the children afterward and brought them up as their own."

"Well, if that's the case, I doubt it was the chauffeur then," Hazel said. "He wouldn't make enough for them to run away together. And I'd rule out Lord Wakefield too. A man of his stature couldn't up and leave all his responsibilities behind. But Thomas, now that's a different story. He would have the funds for such a trip and the freedom to do as he wanted, within reason. Though I suspect his mother wouldn't be too happy about it."

Duffy walked in from outside again, taking off his black cap and running a hand through his messy hair. The breeze had picked up since they'd returned from Farnsworth Abbey and now whistled past the windows. "Still talking about the murder, I see. Well, I'd advise not ruling out Lord Wakefield just yet. Wouldn't be the first time the lord of the manor gets a servant in a delicate way. And he lied about being at the club. Could be he was the one arguing with Doris in his study that night too, maybe about trying to buy her off to keep her silence about the pregnancy."

"True," Shrewsbury said, rubbing his jaw, his expression thoughtful. "But if the motive was jealousy, I'd still advise concentrating on the two younger chaps. Makes more sense they'd be sowing their wild oats versus the older, more established Lord Wakefield. Plus, if the chauffeur was the father, then Thomas could've wanted him gone."

"Or vice versa," Alice added.

"I just don't know about Thomas, though. It doesn't add up that it would be him," Hazel said, straightening. "Mrs. Crosby said he came running up to the third floor shortly after Doris screamed. I doubt he'd have time to push her, get back downstairs, then run up again without being seen by anyone." She sighed and shook her head. "What I really need to do is question the chauffeur, but I can't go back to Farnsworth Abbey again so soon without raising suspicions."

"Ask Inspector Gibson to go," Alice said. "Maybe he can talk to him for you."

"No, I don't want to go to the police with this until I have something more solid to show them." Hazel stood and walked over to stand beside Duffy near the sink. "It's all still a bit too muddled and confusing, and

I do have my pride and investigative reputation to worry about. I'm a mystery novelist, after all. People expect me to know what I'm talking about."

"Well, I can talk to George, my under-butler friend over at the Farnsworth estate, again if you'd like, madam," Duffy offered, twisting his hat in his hands. "Perhaps I can get the chauffeur's timetable and take you over to meet with him when no one's around so you can talk to him. Or, if you'd prefer I do it, I can find out when the family's going out to dinner next time, and meet up with their driver then. Most of us chat to one another while we wait, and I'm pretty well-respected, so I should have a way in with him."

"That second option sounds like a better plan, madam, if you ask me," Shrewsbury added, pushing to his feet as well. "If this other chauffeur is the killer, he's not likely to tell you, is he? Besides, it would put you in danger to speak with him alone. If you go when other drivers are around, at least you'll have some protection."

"I'm perfectly capable of taking care of myself, thank you." Hazel scoffed. "But I suppose you're right. Let's try to find out when the family will be out again and meet up with their driver then, Duffy. Though I'll come around back with you. I'd like to question the man myself and get a feel for if he's lying."

"I'll protect her, don't worry," Duffy said, exchanging a look with Shrewsbury.

"See?" She smiled at the now-glowering butler, appreciating the fact her staff was so protective of her, even if it was a bit unwarranted at the moment. "It will all be fine, I assure you. Don't worry so much, Shrewsbury. Duffy won't let anything happen to me."

## CHAPTER TWELVE

"Are you sure this is where they are?" Hazel said, staring out at Sparrows Restaurant. Hazel hadn't been to the restaurant in years. Not since Charles's death. The Tudor building was homey enough, and even though Hazel enjoyed the atmosphere, she didn't imagine it was quite up to Lady Wakefield's exacting standards. Peering through the window, she noticed both bluebloods and blue-collar workers filling the tables—a highly unusual occurrence but one that was starting to happen more and more.

"Yes, madam," Duffy said, smiling at her from behind the wheel of the Sunbeam as he tipped his hat. "When I was at the pub last night, George told me both Lady Wakefield and Eugenia were lunching here today."

Hazel watched as the crowds bustled past them

and into the entrance of the restaurant. She'd meant what she'd told Shrewsbury earlier, that Duffy would protect her. Still, with the possibility of a murderer on the loose, safety was a top concern. "You'll stay close by, in case I need you."

"Of course, madam." He tipped his hat. "Like I said, the chauffeurs smoke and have a chat while we're waiting. I'll be around the back of the building." Duffy pointed around the corner of the establishment, and Hazel peeked around to see a flock of uniformed young men standing near an array of fine vehicles. "If you want to meet with them as you mentioned yesterday, I'll stay by your side, madam, no question."

Her nerves said no. But her curiosity and dedication to Doris's case said yes. "Okay, if you think it's appropriate. Is Alphonse there?"

"Not sure." Duffy drove around the side of the restaurant and parked near the Wakefields' silver Rolls-Royce. After cutting the engine, he glanced around then leaned over to whisper. "Doesn't look like he's here today, madam. Seems their footman, Davis, drove them today. But I happen to know he's a fan of your books too, madam."

"Oh dear." She allowed Duffy to help her out of the car then followed him over to where a dark-haired young man with tanned skin and an easy smile stood with a couple of other drivers.

"Gentlemen, may I introduce my employer and the famous mystery novelist, Mrs. Hazel Martin." Duffy made the introductions and helped put her at ease by joking about her research and instead of writing about how the butler did it, a future book might have the chauffeur as culprit. The other two drivers wandered off, leaving them alone with Davis, the Wakefields' temporary chauffeur.

"I'm a big fan, Mrs. Martin," Davis said, bowing slightly to her. "Wish I'd known you'd be here. I'd have brought a copy of your last book for you to sign."

Hazel chuckled, cutting through his flattery with the real reason she was there. "Such a tragedy what happened to Doris at Farnsworth Abbey."

"Yes, sad." Davis exhaled a stream of smoke from his cigarette then leaned back against the Rolls, not seeming particularly upset at all about his coworker's recent demise. "That's the way of things, though. Life's hard, and the world is cruel."

Suspicious now, Hazel tried a different angle. "Doris was seen passing notes to Alphonse Ash, the Wakefields' regular chauffeur, while he was in the garage, and then later the two were seen arguing. I've been told Ash also argued with Thomas Wakefield too.

Do you think perhaps Alphonse Ash was more involved with Doris's death than he let on?"

Beside her, Duffy tensed. She'd apparently crossed some unwritten rule of chauffeur conduct, but she couldn't worry about that now. Hazel needed to find out what Davis knew about Alphonse's relationship with Doris, and directness seemed the fastest route.

The man narrowed his gaze on her but remained silent, puffing away on his cigarette.

He might be tight lipped, but Hazel was older and had more tricks up her sleeve. If directness didn't work, perhaps flattery would. It had won over Lady Wakefield, after all, and this man had already confessed to being a fan. Hazel smiled and took the chauffeur by the arm, leading him a short distance away from Duffy. "Tell me what you know about Doris, and I'll share with you some of the details of my newest plot. You'll get the scoop before anyone else."

"Add a shilling to the pot, and you have a deal," he said, stopping her in her tracks. Maybe he wasn't so charming after all. Just greedy. Still, it was a small price to pay for the truth.

Hazel dug a coin out of her beaded black purse and handed it to him. "Were you there when Doris fell?"

"No, I wasn't there." Davis snorted. "I was out driving Lord Wakefield."

Confused, Hazel frowned. Lord Wakefield hadn't been at his club. "Driving him where?"

Davis waggled his fingers for another coin, and Hazel sighed, handing him more money. Maybe she should start calling the man Midas instead of Davis. "Fine. You've been paid. Now tell me... where were you taking Lord Wakefield?"

"You certainly ask a lot of questions," he said, his gaze darting around as if he was having second thoughts about talking to her. He bit both the coins she gave him, testing the metal to be sure they weren't counterfeits, before slipping them into his pocket. He crushed his cigarette out beneath the heel of his black leather boot and crossed his arms. "Are you working with the Old Bill or something?"

Quick on her feet, Hazel fell back on her book as an excuse. "No, I'm not working with the police. As I said, I'm writing a new book and need to verify some information for my research. The Wakefields know I'm writing it too. In fact, there's even going to be a dedication to the family at the front of the book."

Davis sighed and watched her with narrowed eyes for a moment before answering. "Fine. I suppose it's alright, if the family knows, as you say. Lord Wakefield didn't go to his club, like he told the Old Bill. He went to Mrs. Pommel's house on Grove Street. Truth is, he goes there every other Thursday, though I'm not usually the one who takes him. He alternates those visits with his appointments at the club. I drive him to those too sometimes, when Alphonse is otherwise engaged. In fact, I just took him to his club the Thursday before Doris died."

"So he sees Mrs. Pommel?" Hazel said, still snagged on the earlier fact. The widow was known to be very generous with her attentions to various members of the aristocracy. Was Lord Wakefield having an affair with her? If so, then he'd lied about being at the club not because he'd pushed Doris out the window, but because he was visiting his widowed lover across town. She frowned at Davis. "You said you drive the family when Alphonse is otherwise engaged?"

"Yes." He glanced at her purse then back to her.

*Of course.* She dug out a third coin and handed it to him. "And where is Alphonse today? Out driving another member of the Wakefield family somewhere?"

"No idea, madam." Davis shrugged. "Can tell you for a fact he isn't driving the family anywhere anymore, though. Alphonse packed up and left Farnsworth Abbey the morning poor Doris died."

Distracted, Hazel allowed Duffy to escort her back to the front of the restaurant. Her mind was still whirling from what she'd just discovered about the regular chauffeur. Alphonse had to have played a part in this murder somehow, given his abrupt departure, though if he was truly gone before the fall had taken place as Davis had said, then it didn't add up that he was the killer.

For one, Mrs. Crosby had mentioned Alphonse Ash rarely spent time in the main house, which meant he'd be out of place there and people would've definitely noticed his presence.

Secondly, even if he had ventured into the house that day, him being able to get up to the third floor unseen—given the stairs were off the very busy kitchen area—was doubtful at best. And he didn't seem particularly close with any of the other staff, certainly not enough for them to help him cover up the murder of one of their own.

Unfortunately, her conversation with Davis only served to leave her with more questions than answers, but at least she could now rule out Lord Wakefield as a suspect. He'd been with his mistress, not at

Farnsworth. She'd let Detective Gibson know about Davis and have him check out both the driver's alibi and Lord Wakefield's location that night, but it seemed that was one thing she could tick off her list.

"Will you be staying for lunch, madam?" Duffy asked, breaking Hazel out of her musings.

"Oh." She gazed at their menu tacked to the wall near the door and saw they had a special watercress salad that day. She did so love a good watercress salad. Her stomach rumbled, and Hazel smiled. "Actually, I think I will. Return for me in an hour, please."

"Yes, madam." Duffy tipped his hat and disappeared back around the corner while Hazel headed inside.

The interior was small, with exposed wood and a clean, shiny pine floor. A large stone fireplace crackled in one corner, and against the opposite wall was a carved wooden bar with an assortment of spirits and wines lining shelves on the wall behind it.

The place had been one of her Charles's favorite haunts, and she spotted several of the other local bobbies in one corner near the front of the restaurant. Thankfully, though, no Inspector Gibson. She had enough to deal with today without him too. Her eyes adjusted to the dimmer light, and she spotted Lady

Wakefield and Eugenia at a small table across the room.

"Good day, madam," the waitress said. "One today?"

"Yes, please." She followed the woman to a corner table, straining to hear the conversation as she passed close by the Wakefields' table.

"...borrow that lovely black sable stole you just bought," Eugenia said to her mother.

"I'm sorry, my dear, but that's quite impossible," Lady Wakefield said. "I'm afraid it was damaged in storage."

"What?" Eugenia frowned, still pale but looking a tad livelier than she had the previous morning. "But I thought you had Mrs. Crosby take all the furs out of storage days ago. That stole was brand new. I hope you're going to..."

"Here we are, madam." The waitress held Hazel's chair for her then handed her a menu. "I'll be back to take your order."

As she perused the selections, Hazel couldn't help connecting the snippets of the exchange she'd overheard between the Wakefield ladies with what she already knew. Doris had reportedly been planning a trip up north. Now those two were discussing fur coats. Had Doris been going north with Eugenia and not her lover?

If Eugenia wanted to borrow her mother's stole, perhaps she was still planning on heading north, despite Doris's demise. Mrs. Crosby had mentioned seeing Thomas at the train station as well that day. Could her brother be planning to leave with her? The twins were exceptionally close, after all. And it would get him out of the sticky situation with the Tewkesbury girl too. Hazel had originally assumed the trip would have been cancelled after Doris's death, but perhaps not.

She glanced at them over the top of her menu, only to see them watching her and waving. Soon, Lady Wakefield and Eugenia were at Hazel's side.

"Ah, Mrs. Martin. We meet again," Lady Wakefield said. "Such a lovely day outside."

"Yes, it is." Hazel smiled. "What are you both doing today? Are you planning a trip?"

"Oh, no," Eugenia said, her response a bit too quick. "Nothing like that."

"Something much more mundane, I fear," Lady Wakefield said. "With winter coming, it's time to get the rest of my furs out of storage. I had Mrs. Crosby get some of them about a week ago, so I decided to get the rest of them myself today. A trip does sound nice, though. Maybe once we put all this dreadful business with Doris behind us we can plan an excursion." She stroked her daughter's hair and frowned. "That might help my Eugenia to return to good health. She's so delicate these days, and I'm hoping to make a good match for her with the Earl of Whitborough, if he takes an interest in her. Which won't happen if she's not feeling her best."

Eugenia gave her mother an irritated look that Hazel didn't miss.

It seemed she wasn't interested in this earl in the least.

So both twins were unhappy with their arranged matches.

Lady Wakefield continued, apparently unaware of her daughter's glare. "As I said, I'm just worried about the scandal surrounding the death and its investigation, both on the family name and on my children's marriage prospects. I sincerely hope it will all blow over before my daughter's reputation is ruined."

"Well, I'm sure things will work out in the end. They always do." Hazel smiled at the waitress who'd re-appeared at her side then ordered her salad and a pot of tea.

"We'll let you get back to your lunch then, Mrs.

Martin," Eugenia said, tugging her mother's arm. "Have a lovely afternoon."

"Yes." Lady Wakefield pulled free from her daughter's hold. "We still need to discuss that acknowledgement in your next book. Shall we set up an appointment to do that now?"

Much as Hazel wanted to visit Farnsworth again, she didn't want to do so under Lady Wakefield's watchful eye. "Unfortunately, I'm so busy with deadlines for my publisher over the next few days, I'll need to check my calendar before I commit to anything. May I ring you once I get home?"

"Certainly." Lady Wakefield smiled, apparently satisfied for now. "I look forward to it."

"Me too." The ladies said their goodbyes and headed back to their table, leaving Hazel alone at last. She waited until they'd left the restaurant before she sat back and released her pent-up breath.

As she stirred sugar into her tea, Hazel couldn't help dwelling on Eugenia's reaction to her mother's news about the earl. Most women would be excited at the prospect of marrying into old money. And the earl, while bookish, wasn't awful looking either. He would've made a good match for a girl like Eugenia.

Then she remembered the girl's nervous answer when Hazel had inquired about a trip. Between the news that Alphonse had run off right before Doris's death and now Eugenia acting secretly about the supposed trip up north with her brother, it certainly made Thomas look guiltier of pushing poor Doris, that was for sure.

## CHAPTER THIRTEEN

Later that afternoon, Hazel was back in the kitchen at Hastings Manor, helping Alice and Maggie bake strawberry jam tarts. Lots and lots of tarts.

"Why so many?" Hazel asked as she slid yet another baking sheet full of them into the oven. "There's enough here to feed the entire Royal Air Force."

Alice shrugged and set the timer. "Well, madam, I'm just being prepared, in case you need an excuse to visit Inspector Gibson again soon. What with your snooping and all."

Hazel shook her head, both at the comment and the fact her once feline-wary cook had now set out a bowl of cream for Dickens just inside the kitchen door-way. The cat was hunched over it, lapping away. Hazel bit back a smile, nodded toward the dish, and raised a brow. "Looks like you two have become quite close."

"Nonsense." Alice huffed. "I just know that bowl of cream keeps him occupied and out of my way in the kitchen. It's common sense, that's all. As my mother always said, you catch more flies with honey."

"Right." Hazel took a seat at the table to wait for the tarts to finish baking, and her thoughts once more turned to her investigation. "My 'snooping,' as you called it, turned out to be quite productive today. I had an interesting conversation with the Wakefields' interim chauffeur before lunch behind the restaurant."

Alice tsked as she wiped down the counters. "You, hanging out behind restaurants, putting yourself in danger. What would Mr. Charles have said about that?"

"Well, considering he enjoyed me helping him on cases, I'd think he'd be proud of me," Hazel replied, stretching out her legs. She'd worn a new pair of burgundy satin flat shoes to match the maroon flowers on her white cotton day dress, but the wretched things weren't exactly comfy, and now her feet were sore. "Besides, Duffy was by my side the whole time, as promised. I was completely and perfectly safe."

"Really, madam?" Maggie sat beside her at the table, wiping her flour-covered hands on the front of her apron. "Did this new driver say what happened to Alphonse?"

"Seems he left the day Doris died. No one knows why or where he went."

"Sounds fishy to me," Alice said, hands on hips. "Like he wanted to run away from something."

"Or someone." Hazel toyed with a saltshaker sitting on the table. "I saw Eugenia and Lady Wakefield when I went inside for lunch too. Eugenia seemed unusually nervous when I asked her about them going on a trip."

"Do you think that argument between Thomas and Alphonse had anything to do with his leaving?" Alice asked. "Maybe Thomas threatened him."

"I wondered the same thing." Hazel squinted at the crystal shaker while the cook bustled about, removing a batch of cooled tarts from their tray and putting them into a nice basket. Maggie stood to help. "I also considered the possibility that the twins were still planning to take the trip north anyway, even without Doris. Lady Wakefield seems dead set on getting them married off as soon as possible whether they like their potential spouses or not."

"Hmm." Alice harrumphed. "Begging your pardon, madam, but you higher classes are a strange lot. Never works well when you marry for money and not love. I know that's the way it's always been done, but that don't make it right." She double-checked the timer then took a seat on the other side of Hazel. "Wouldn't blame those two if they did run away. Still doesn't explain poor Doris, though."

"Are you still thinking this surrounding her death all has to do with the baby then, madam?" Maggie asked. "Though we still don't know who was the father."

"I think it had something to do with the pregnancy, yes. A crime of passion seems most likely at this point," Hazel said. "My money is currently on the chauffeur. Thomas was seen in a tête-à-tête with Doris, and he argued with Alphonse. Maybe she was having Thomas's baby, so Doris broke things off with the chauffeur. I mean who wouldn't choose the son of a lord over a member of staff?"

"True," Alice said, crossing her arms. "But I wouldn't write off Lord Wakefield just yet either. He could've pushed that poor maid just as easily as some jilted lover. Or it could've been someone else we haven't even identified yet."

"Alphonse couldn't have killed Doris, unless his leaving was some elaborate ruse and he came back to push her over. But even then, his appearance in the house would've caused a stir, since he was in there so infrequently. Though in an odd way, I suppose that makes perfect sense, because it gives Alphonse an alibi. But I'm not sure jealousy is a strong enough motive to kill Doris. And I learned today that it couldn't have been Lord Wakefield either. The temporary chauffeur told me he was across town at Mrs. Pommel's house on Grove Street at the time of the murder. Drove the lord there himself. So, really, that just leaves Thomas."

Alice tsked. "He was such a nice young boy too."

"That explains why Lady Wakefield lied about being in her sewing room and able to see Lord Wakefield in his study. She likely didn't want the scandal about him and Mrs. Pommel getting out," Hazel said. She grabbed a notebook and pencil from a nearby drawer and sketched out a rough layout of Farnsworth Abbey. "Here's my sticking point with that theory, though." She pointed to locations on her crude map as she spoke. "Mrs. Crosby was here in the dining room when she heard Doris's scream. Betsy stated she was in the library at the time of the fall. Mrs. Crosby's statement corroborates Betsy's alibi because she said she saw Betsy run past the dining room doorway from the direction of the library and she then followed the maid upstairs to the third floor. There's no other way to get to that turret room except through the back stairs that lead up from the kitchen. Mrs. Crosby also stated she passed Lady Wakefield coming down the stairs as she was going up. Lady Wakefield said she'd already been to the turret room and was descending the stairs as she and Betsy ran toward the third floor. Everyone else was already in the turret room when they got upstairs or were down on the ground below where poor Doris landed. Mrs. Crosby said Thomas arrived on the third floor right behind her."

"Huh." Alice frowned, staring at Hazel's map. "Well, if that's true, then it couldn't really be Thomas either, could it? I mean there's no way he'd have been able to push Doris, get downstairs, then get back up to the turret room that fast, and he'd have passed some of the staff on the way, right?"

"Was there another escape route from the turret room that no one's found yet?" Maggie asked.

"No, there isn't another way down. I checked the last time I was at the estate." Hazel scowled, going over all the known facts in her head again. "And the killer couldn't have taken the same stairs from the kitchen without being seen. It had to be someone who wasn't in the turret room or on the ground floor afterward who pushed Doris, because there's only one place on the third floor to hide. Whoever killed Doris must have concealed themselves in the attic."

"Well, then." Alice crossed her arms. "If that's the case, then it very well could've been Alphonse Ash. Perhaps he only pretended to leave the morning before then hid out in that attic, waiting for his chance. He wouldn't have been seen in the room or on the ground floor since he'd already left. And no one would notice him missing because no one would've expected him there to begin with."

"Or it could have been someone we've not yet suspected." Hazel straightened as realization dawned. "Thomas and Lady Wakefield were both seen on the stairs. Eugenia was in the house, but I was told she stayed in her room the whole time. But maybe she didn't. Maybe *she* pushed Doris. It would've taken some elaborate planning on her part and perfect timing, but it could have been done. She would've had to go through the kitchen when it was empty and sneak into the attic to wait until everyone had left the turret room afterward and still somehow manage to be downstairs in her own room again before she was discovered. It could be done, I suppose."

The more she thought about it, though, the less it made sense, especially given Eugenia's current health conditions. The poor girl didn't look strong enough to lift a fork, let alone push another person off a roof. She pursed her lips. "But she's been very ill lately, which would've slowed her reflexes, and given the fact the family's quarters are on the other side of that massive house and Eugenia's frail physical state, it doesn't seem likely."

The ladies stared at Hazel's drawing in silence for a moment, pondering.

"Wait a minute," Alice said, snapping her fingers and smiling. "You said Lord Wakefield was at Grove Street according to that interim chauffeur, but what if the lord doubled back after he was dropped off and used Grove Street as his alibi?"

"Then why would he lie to the police and about being at his club?" Hazel countered.

"He might've had to say that if the Old Bill asked him his whereabouts in front of Lady Wakefield, but he wouldn't use the club as an alibi because it's full of people he knew. Someone would notice if he left. That house on Grove Street only contains one person—Mrs. Pommel. It's a lot easier to get one person to lie for you versus a whole room of them."

"True." Hazel sighed. "But we still need to establish a better motive for the killer. Was Doris murdered to keep her quiet or because of a lovers' quarrel?"

"The maid Betsy said she heard an argument between Doris and another person in Lord Wakefield's study, right, madam?" Maggie said. "Maybe that's our clue."

"Possibly. It happened a week before the murder, so Alphonse would've still been employed at Farnsworth and present at the estate. But I can't imagine it would've been him and Doris fighting in Lord Wakefield's study. How would two servants alone get into that wing, especially one who rarely visited the house to begin with, without Betsy, or anyone else, noticing? And it couldn't have been the lord and Doris arguing either, since the chauffeur today also told me that Lord Wakefield has a standing appointment at his club every other Thursday and he'd taken him that night too instead of Alphonse, so Lord Wakefield wasn't there at the time of the fight."

"Could it have been Doris and Thomas then, in the study?" Maggie asked.

"That would make sense, madam," Alice added. "Especially since you mentioned Doris using the words 'not paid off.'" The cook frowned. "Except why would Thomas want to buy Doris off if he was planning to run away with her and his child?"

"Good question." Hazel pushed to her feet. "I wonder if that argument had anything to do with Alphonse's abrupt disappearance."

"Could be, madam." Alice turned and grabbed the

basket of tarts then shoved it into Hazel's hands. "Sounds like that missing chauffeur might just be the key. And since he's gone and we don't have the proper resources here at Hastings Manor to find and question him, seems you need to make another visit to Inspector Gibson's flat. See? I told you all these tarts would come in handy."

## CHAPTER FOURTEEN

An hour later, on her way to the front door, Shrewsbury stopped Hazel.

"Pardon me, madam," he said, blocking her path. He stood a good foot taller than her, but she'd never found his height imposing, though she supposed it could be under the right circumstances. He held her coat for her once more while she slipped her arms into the sleeves. "But I couldn't help overhearing part of your conversation with Alice."

Hazel bit her lips to hide her smile. He was always so formal, it was hard to picture her stuffy butler with his ear pressed to the wall, eavesdropping. "You did, did you?"

"Yes, madam." He frowned and clasped his hands behind his back, his black uniform and white shirt pristine as always. "Not due to listening, mind you. I was busy in the wine cellar, and voices carry down the pipes." She had her suspicions he wasn't being entirely honest with her—especially given the fact her Charles used to rave about the man's spying skills—but she refrained from saying so. Shrewsbury seemed uncharacteristically talkative tonight, and she wanted to take advantage of such a rare event by listening. "I might be able to assist you in getting information from the Wakefields' chauffeur, Alphonse Ash, ma'am."

"Really? How?"

"I have ways that are faster and"—he cleared his throat, fisting his hands at his sides—"more *effective* than the police."

Her eyes widened slightly. She adjusted the basket on her arm and narrowed her gaze. She'd always suspected there was more to her butler than met the eye, but she'd never imagined he had skills in boxing as well. And yes, she was heading over to talk to Inspector Gibson—Michael—again, but it couldn't hurt to have the butler put out feelers as well. "Fine, Shrewsbury. Do your best."

She took the burgundy cloche hat he handed her and slid it into place over her hair, checking her appearance in the mirror before heading outside, where Duffy waited with the Sunbeam. Going to see Michael now was good. She'd promised to fill the

Inspector in on whatever she learned during her investigations, plus she wanted to maintain that relationship for future cases. The last thing she wanted was for Gibson to think she was holding back clues.

Twenty minutes later, Duffy pulled up in front of Michael's flat again, and this time Hazel had no hesitancy as she walked to the front door. The same landlady answered and let her in, and she quickly made it up to Michael's door. He answered on her first knock.

"Hazel, so good to see you again." He gestured for her to come in, his gaze snagging on the basket over her arm. "What brings you here today?"

"Alice made an extra batch of strawberry jam tarts." She held up the basket then set it on his kitchen table, noticing once more how clean and tidy everything was. "So I thought I'd bring some over to you. And perhaps we could discuss the case some more."

"Perfect." He pulled back the gingham fabric covering the goodies and inhaled. The rich berry smell surrounded Hazel too, and she was glad she'd had two of the tarts herself before coming to his flat. Otherwise she might've had to partake of his stash of goodies. "I always love Alice's baking." Michael smiled, and Hazel's toes curled just a bit in her pretty red shoes. "But where's Dickens? I thought we agreed you'd bring him along the next time you came."

"Oh." She bit her lip. She'd forgotten about the cat in her haste to get here and discuss Doris's case. "Well, he was napping in his favorite chair, and I didn't want to disturb him. He's quite content now that Alice serves him a bowl of cream in our kitchen each day."

"Ah, well, I can't say I blame him then. I'd be in heaven too if a woman pampered me that way. Would you like some tea?" he asked, shuffling his feet, things between them feeling a bit awkward now. " A great accompaniment to the tarts."

"Tea would be lovely, thank you. But no tarts for me. I've already had mine before I came." She gave him a small smile then headed into his living room, where yet another fire crackled merrily in the fireplace. She'd always imagined bachelors weren't quite so careful with their surroundings, but Michael seemed to have a place for everything. She liked that. Hazel took a seat on a Victorian chair and crossed her ankles, her hands clasped in her lap. "I've, um, got some new information on the case."

"Oh?" Michael leaned his head around the door to the kitchen. "Please tell me. I can hear you in here."

"Alright." Talking about Doris's pregnancy with a single man hardly seemed polite, even if Michael already knew. Call her old-fashioned, but she just couldn't do it in mixed company. So, instead, she said,

"Turns out Lord Wakefield really did have an alibi. He was at Grove Street with Mrs. Pommel, at least according to their temporary chauffeur."

"Yes," Michael said, carrying in a tray holding a small teapot, cups and saucers, two plates with a tart each, forks, spoons, and napkins. He set it all out on a low table between them then took a seat across from Hazel while she poured their tea. "He came clean to us about that too finally, once we started digging deeper into Doris's death. I've confirmed he was at Grove Street at the time of the murder."

"Hmm," she said as she stirred sugar into her tea. "I also believe Eugenia Wakefield knows more about what happened than she's letting on."

"Agreed." Michael bit into his tart then sighed with pleasure. "I haven't been able to question her yet, though. She's not technically a suspect, and that mother of hers hovers around her like a protective Pekingese."

Hazel chuckled at the apt description.

Michael swallowed another mouthful of tart then wiped his mouth before continuing. "I'm guessing whatever Eugenia knows has something to do with Doris and her brother, Thomas. There've been several witnesses reporting the two of them being seen together outside of the family residence. Though if they were involved romantically, it hardly makes sense to me that Thomas would kill her, unless they had some sort of fight."

"Yes. I find the disappearance of their regular chauffeur troubling as well. Seems Alphonse Ash disappeared before Doris died. And all of this after the argument Betsy, the Wakefields' maid, overheard between Thomas and Alphonse. I've heard Doris also fought with the man."

"I wonder how that ties in to the rest." Michael polished off the last piece of his tart, while Hazel's still sat untouched. "Are you sure you're not going to eat yours?"

"Oh, no. Honestly, I filled up on them back at Hastings Manor. Please keep it for yourself for later." Hazel smiled. "Perhaps you should look into where this chauffeur might have gone after he left Farnsworth Abbey."

"Yes, I think I should."

Hazel watched him over the rim of her cup as he cleared away the rest of the dishes and took them back to the kitchen. "So we know that Doris was going away on a trip. Maybe whoever killed her didn't want her to leave."

"Or," Michael said, returning to the living room to take his seat once more, "they didn't know she was leaving and wanted to silence her about something. If she had information to blackmail someone with, someone in a position to lose a lot if she talked, they might not want to have that hanging over their heads."

"Possibly. But one thing still bothers me about all this," Hazel said. "Why hasn't the father of Doris's child come forward?"

"Father?" Michael frowned, sitting back in his chair. "What child?"

"The baby. Doris was pregnant." Hazel blinked at him, astonished. "Surely the autopsy must have shown that."

Michael shook his head, his dark brows knitted. "Wherever did you get that idea? If anything, the autopsy proved Doris was most definitely *not* pregnant."

## CHAPTER FIFTEEN

Gobsmacked by Michael's revelation, Hazel didn't say much on the journey back to Hastings Manor. In fact, it wasn't until she and Duffy walked into the kitchen that she found her voice again. She waited until Alice and Maggie were present before she spoke. "Doris wasn't pregnant. The autopsy proved it."

Duffy scowled. "But if she wasn't with child, then why did the murderer want to silence her?"

"Oh dear. Well, maybe our original love-triangle theory's correct then, madam," Alice said, crossing her arms. "One lover gets jealous, decides if he can't have her, no one can."

"I'm just not sure anymore." Hazel draped her coat over a chair and put her hat on the seat before slumping down into a second chair, toeing off her red shoes then sighing with relief. "Michael did verify that Lord Wakefield was at Grove Street at the time of Doris's murder, so it couldn't have been him. But we still don't know who she was arguing with in the study that night, unless it was Thomas."

"But madam, you said Thomas couldn't have pushed her because he was on the stairs that night behind Mrs. Crosby," Maggie said, taking Hazel's hat and coat.

"So it must be Alphonse Ash then?" Alice mused, her gaze narrowed.

"That would explain why he ran," Duffy added. "The coward."

"And Thomas won the argument with Ash, and that was presumably over Doris." Maggie leaned her elbow on the table, her expression thoughtful. "If Doris had spurned him for Thomas, that could have made Alphonse angry. Perhaps even angry enough to double back and kill Doris so Thomas couldn't have her."

"And if Lady Wakefield was set on matching Thomas up with a member of the aristocracy, then he might have seen that his only way out was to take Doris away up north. To get away from his mother," Alice said.

"Yes, but there are still things that don't fit. Like if

Doris wasn't with child, why in the world would she buy that pregnancy corset at Lady Etienne's?" Hazel shook her head. "Those things are expensive. That makes no sense."

"Wait! It *does* make sense." Alice held up her index finger. "It makes sense if she was faking a pregnancy to extort money!"

Duffy looked skeptical. "From Ash? I doubt he'd have any cash worth taking, being just a chauffeur." He glanced sideways at Hazel, looking a bit guilty. "Sorry, madam. No offense, but us drivers don't make much."

Hazel made a mental note to give Duffy a raise at her earliest convenience. "Maybe the killer fell for Doris's ruse and thought she really was pregnant with Lord Wakefield's or Thomas's child. If it was Alphonse and he loved her, he could have killed her in a jealous rage."

"Or perhaps the chauffeur was out of the picture altogether. Perhaps it was one of the Wakefield family she was trying to blackmail by pretending they got her pregnant. The blackmail angle would explain the argument Betsy overheard."

"No, it wouldn't," Maggie said, her tone emphatic. "Betsy said she overheard Doris say she wouldn't be paid off. She would never have taken money from something so wicked."

Hazel considered all the facts. "Betsy did tell me she couldn't hear the conversation very well. I wonder if Doris perhaps added more to the conversation she couldn't hear, like 'for such a small sum' or if she misheard entirely. Only one thing's certain. I need to talk to Betsy again and see if she can remember any more about that conversation."

"Well, I can probably arrange that for you, madam," Maggie said. "Though I still have a hard time believing the Doris I knew could be so devious. And I thought that corset was meant to conceal a baby, not fool people into thinking you had one on the way."

"Good point, though I have no idea, honestly," Hazel said. "I don't wear corsets, I'm afraid."

"Well, I used to." Alice sighed. "Back in my younger days. And I don't know about these newfangled kind, mind you, but Maggie's right. They are usually made to hold you in. There is a bit of leeway, though, for expansion, so maybe Doris could've stuffed a small pillow or something under there to make it appear she was with child."

"I need to check with that shop assistant again, maybe even talk to the owner." Hazel glanced at the clock on the wall. "But it's too late now. All the shops are closed. I'll go back to Lady Etienne's first thing tomorrow and find out for sure."

"If you'll excuse me then, madam"—Maggie pushed to her feet and headed toward the door—"I'll just put away your coat and hat then go over to the Hen and Bull and see if Betsy's there so I can arrange your meeting."

"Certainly," Hazel said, leaning back in her chair and stretching out her legs, glad to be done for the day. But no sooner had the maid left than Shrewsbury walked in, his expression concerned.

"I have news about Alphonse Ash, ma'am," he said, slipping out of his black wool topper. "One of my contacts has located him working at the stables of Lord Bowker's country estate."

"That certainly was fast," Hazel said, impressed. "Your contacts are quite something."

"I have my ways, madam." The butler shrugged, giving her a hint of a proud smile.

"Any idea how long Ash has been there or when he arrived?" Hazel asked, straightening. "Has anyone questioned him yet?"

"No one's talked to him in person yet, madam. Once he heard the police were looking for him, he ran. But the head groom has been questioned, madam, and he said Ash was employed there since noon last Thursday. Seems he arranged for the job earlier in the month."

Hazel frowned. "He ran when the police tried to find him for questioning, which implies guilt. And if he arranged for that job ahead of time, then he was already planning on leaving. Perhaps he did that on purpose, knowing he was going to kill Doris."

"Indeed, madam." Shrewsbury nodded, clasping his hands behind his back. "But I'm afraid Alphonse Ash can't be the killer. Lord Bowker's estate is a good three hours from Farnsworth Abbey, even with a car. And others have verified his presence in the stables until nearly midnight on that Thursday when Doris was killed."

"Blimey." Alice slumped back against the table's edge, her expression disappointed. "That means we're back to blackmail then."

"No." Hazel frowned. "It couldn't have been Lord Wakefield or Thomas either. We deduced earlier that Thomas wouldn't have had time to push Doris then get back downstairs to come back up again behind Mrs. Crosby, and Lord Wakefield has an alibi."

"Drat. You're right, madam." Alice sighed. "Maybe there's a secret passageway?"

"I doubt it." Hazel straightened. "But there is another possibility. One that I brought up earlier but then dismissed. There's another person who was very close to both Thomas and Doris and who would've known about the trip. And that person wasn't in the room or on the ground floor when Doris was pushed, either. Eugenia."

# CHAPTER SIXTEEN

Hazel tossed and turned most of the night, Doris's case running through her head over and over. The clues did not add up to Eugenia, no matter how she fit them together.

By the time she got out of bed before dawn and got ready for the day, Dickens was at her bedside, eager for his breakfast. She scooped him up and put him on the bed beside her, using him as a sounding board for her ideas.

"It doesn't make sense, boy. Why would Eugenia kill Doris, huh?" She stroked his head and laughed when he purred loudly. "If Thomas loved Doris, then Eugenia wouldn't want her brother to be unhappy. Unless she did it for Thomas. But why would he want her to?"

From everything Lady Wakefield had said to

Hazel, the twins were conspiring together, not fighting. In fact, maybe they were the ones going away on the trip, not Doris. Maybe they were taking a trip to try to escape their mother's oppressive attempts at match-making and were bringing Doris along as a helper or sidekick. But that still left out many important pieces of the puzzle.

She exhaled slowly and leaned back on the mattress, propping herself up on one elbow while Dickens stretched out beside her, rolling onto his back for a tummy rub. Her bedroom looked much the same as it had when Charles had been alive—same large brass bed, same ornate carved mahogany dresser and matching mirror that she'd inherited along with Hastings Manor, same pastel painted French doors leading into the attached bath with the white claw-foot tub.

Nostalgia and loneliness blended inside her. This room, more than any other, reminded her of her Charles and made her miss having his constant companionship beside her, his soapy clean cedar smell, his gentle smile.

She took a deep breath and shook off the memories, focusing on her current dilemma. "Then Thomas fought with Alphonse, and Alphonse left. Presumably that means Thomas won Doris, right?" She ran her finger absently through the cat's silky silver-beige fur, her mind whirling a million miles a second. "Eugenia might have been jealous of all the attention Doris was getting from her brother, I suppose. But that doesn't really ring true if she and Doris were as close as everyone said. If that were the case, and she was that close to both of them, then I'd think she would've been happy to see her friend and her brother so happy together."

Frowning, she flopped back onto her pillows. "But there's still the matter of that pregnancy corset. What if Doris faked the pregnancy to hook Thomas and then when he found out, he got mad and killed her? Or maybe Eugenia became annoyed on his behalf and did Doris in, despite their friendship?" She flung her hand over her eyes and groaned. "Oh, Dickens. I just don't know anymore. This whole thing still doesn't seem right, but I don't know what I'm missing."

Dickens meowed loudly and pawed the fringe on a nearby dress. Hazel squinted at the silken strands, realizing they looked very much like corset strings. As if to emphasize his point, the feline leapt up and batted the dress until it fell to the floor. Then he jumped down and scrambled under the bed, still occasionally batting the dangling fringe from under the bed skirt.

Hazel sat up, frowning. Not because her new evening gown was on the floor, but because realization had finally struck. "Yes! Of course, the corset. If I can discover why Doris would want to fool everyone into thinking she was pregnant, then I should have my answer. That's it." Excited to finally be on the right track, she stood, only to halt as a new idea took hold. "Unless..."

She teased the cat out from under the bed then picked him up, kissing the top of his head. "You are truly a genius, aren't you, my Dickens?"

Dickens purred loudly and snuggled in under her chin.

After putting away the cream evening gown, she chose a crisp white-and-pale-blue-striped linen day dress with a matching pair of shoes and a straw brimmed hat for the day. Considering autumn was upon them, this would likely be the last opportunity she had to wear such a summery outfit that year. The sun was rising outside her window as she dressed and did her hair then slid her feet into her shoes and grabbed her handbag. She kissed Dickens once more before rushing downstairs to find Duffy, calling to him over her shoulder. "You be a good boy for Mummy this morning, and I'll bring you a treat back from town after I visit Lady Etienne's again."

# CHAPTER SEVENTEEN

Downstairs, Hazel collected her wool coat from Shrewsbury then ducked her head into the kitchen to let Alice know she wouldn't be in for breakfast that morning. "I'm having Duffy run me back to Lady Etienne's so I can hopefully get more information about that blasted corset and why in the world Doris would be buying it if she wasn't pregnant."

"Good luck, madam," Alice said, pausing in kneading dough for bread later on. "With luck, this case will be solved soon and things can get back to normal."

"Oh, madam," Maggie said, rushing in. "I didn't get a chance to tell you, but I met with a friend who introduced me to the Wakefields' maid Betsy last night. She said she'll be out in the rose gardens near the back of the Farnsworth property this morning to scrub the birdbath. She said that would be a good time for you to speak to her again as there won't be anyone else around, madam."

"Perfect." She stopped by the kitchen door and grabbed a pair of Charles's old black wellies to cover her pristine white shoes. "I'll have Duffy swing by there before we head into town. Thank you, Maggie."

Fifteen minutes later, Hazel had Duffy stop near the forest at the edge of the Farnsworth estate near the rose gardens where Maggie had arranged the meeting for her with Betsy. There was a lovely wrought-iron fence lining the garden, and she smiled as she pulled her late husband's oversized boots on over her shoes. It wasn't particularly muddy since it hadn't rained here in ages, but she didn't want to take any chances with her new wardrobe. With her coat pulled tight around her, Hazel waited until Duffy helped her from the vehicle then made her way over to the fenced-in area. There, just beyond the gate, stood Betsy, scrubbing a large ornate cement birdbath, as promised. She waved the maid over.

"Madam," Betsy said, wiping her hands on the front of her apron then dropping into a quick curtsy. "Maggie said you wanted to speak with me again?"

"Yes, thank you." Hazel batted away an errant clumsy bumblebee that had somehow managed to survive this late in the season. Most of the insects were dead by mid-September. "I wondered if you could clarify for me again exactly what you heard the night of Doris's argument in Lord Wakefield's study. Are you sure she said, 'not paid off'?"

"Yes, madam." Betsy glanced around to make sure no one was listening then stepped closer. "That's exactly what I heard. And that's all she said too. I didn't hear anything else."

"And you still don't have any idea who it was exactly she was arguing with?"

"No, madam."

"You're positive it was the Thursday prior to Doris's death and the time the fight occurred was just before dinner?"

"Thursday prior, that's correct, madam. And I'm sure about that time because, as I said, that's when I go there to dust the books in the library. Same time, same day, every week. That way I don't disturb the family's reading time."

"Right." Hazel exhaled slowly and tapped her fingertips against the cool metal of the fence. There had to be more that happened that night. She just needed to find out what it was. "Tell me about what happened the night Doris died. What do you remember?"

"Well, madam, like I said, at that time every Thursday I'm in the library, dusting the books. Next thing I knew, I heard a scream then the pounding footsteps as everybody ran to see what was going on. I headed straight for the back stairs in the kitchen, since that's the direction the scream came from. I immediately thought something might've happened in the turret room since that's the only way to access that section of the house, and, well, that whole space scares me. So dusty and gloomy up there."

"Was Mrs. Crosby in the dining room when you ran past on your way to the kitchen?" Hazel asked, hoping to corroborate the other woman's story.

"Yes, madam. I remember running past her, but I didn't slow down because the situation seemed so urgent. I knew it would take her longer to get there since she was older, so I went on ahead to see if I could help."

"I see. And when you reached the kitchen, who was in there?"

"The cook and her staff," Betsy said.

"Were any of the Wakefield family members present?"

"No, madam."

"And when you reached the third floor, who did

you see?" Hazel pulled a small notebook from her pocket to jot things down.

"Let's see. Mr. Donovan, the estate manager, George, the under-butler, and Harrison, the butler, were already in the turret room by the time I got there, madam. Then Mrs. Crosby and Mr. Thomas came up the stairs right behind me. From where I was standing, I could see into the turret room, and the window was open, but I... well, I didn't go any farther to look out, madam."

"What about Miss Eugenia?" Hazel looked up from her notepad. "Where was she?"

"I didn't see her, madam. But Mary said Miss Eugenia was in the privy at the time. She's very delicate. Because of her sensitivities, Mary said she made sure she didn't come out to see Doris that way. They were so close, after all. It would have devastated her."

Unfortunately, this conversation had provided her with nothing new, only the same information about how close the two women were. Hazel sighed and put her pad away. "Is there anything else you remember about that night, Betsy? Anything at all that might help us catch Doris's killer?"

"No, madam. I'm sorry I wasn't more help."

"You have been an enormous help, Betsy." Hazel smiled. "Thank you for talking to me again."

The maid curtsied once more then went back to her birdbath while Hazel carefully made her way across the deeply grooved roadway back to the Sunbeam. The clunky boots made walking awkward, but they'd done their job and protected her outfit, which was good. Duffy was waiting and helped her into the passenger seat then walked around to climb behind the wheel again.

"Where to now, madam?" Duffy asked, tipping his hat to her.

"Lady Etienne's, please."

Half an hour later, she was in town once more and marching up to the front door of the tiny shop again, sans boots. From the outside, the shop looked quite attractive, with pastel-pink-and-white awnings over the sparkling display windows and crisp gold lettering on the glass. But inside... well, that was a different story.

It wasn't that the merchandise wasn't top quality. From the talk she'd heard, Lady Etienne's only used the finest Parisian silks and laces in their...products. But still. Thirty-eight years and not one foot in that scandalous establishment, and now two visits in one week. This time she didn't hesitate, just opened the door and made a beeline directly for the shop owner. Filigreed wrought-iron racks of tiny lingerie swirled around her.

"Ah, back again," the same assistant who'd helped her the other day said as Hazel approached. She was wearing the same drab brown cotton dress with the same tape measure around her neck. It seemed the decadence of the lingerie didn't extend to the employees' uniforms. "What may I help you with today?"

"I had a few more questions about that pregnancy corset we discussed the last time I was in the shop." She gestured for the petite French woman to follow her to a more secluded corner of the store, away from the few other patrons who were milling about. "What I would like to know is if such a corset could be used for faking a pregnancy."

"Oh, well." The woman frowned. "That's not what that garment is intended for at all. But I suppose if one was desperate..." Her voice trailed off, and her dark brows knitted, her round face scrunching into a frown. "You know, come to think of it, that maid did purchase an odd size. I knew by looking at her that it would not fit her properly, and I told her so—because the proportions were all wrong. It would have gapped in the waist area, even with a growing infant inside her. But perhaps, if she was using it for the purpose you suggest, then the extra room would be welcome."

"And she didn't mention anything further about the corset or why she wanted it?" Hazel asked.

"No. It was rather odd." The woman glanced at a patron who brushed past them then leaned in closer to Hazel. "As I said, she rushed off without the receipt. I'd seen her walk past earlier with Lady Wakefield, and I didn't want there to be any problems with household monies and a lack of receipt, so later I had the receipt delivered to Farnsworth Abbey. With the corset being the wrong size and all, I guessed she might need it in case of a return. The poor dear was in such a hurry that day. She seemed very flustered and upset. I take it the pregnancy was not a blessing?"

"That's what I'm trying to figure out," Hazel said, shaking her head as she headed for the front door.

## CHAPTER EIGHTEEN

After her two morning meetings, Hazel returned to Hastings Manor more confused than ever. Her investigation into Doris's death was stuck, and she knew of only one way to push it forward—working on her next book. Something about working through revisions and plot twists always got her juices flowing. She went upstairs to her writing room, Dickens close on her heels, and flipped through the manuscript from the beginning.

"Oh dear," she said to the cat. "We mustn't forget to add the acknowledgment. Lady Wakefield will be very upset with us if we do that. She's so determined for her family name to get the recognition it deserves."

Dickens meowed loudly.

"And she's so concerned with how things look. Nothing improper, nothing unseemly."

Another meow.

Dickens jumped from his favorite chair where he was sitting on to the windowsill nearby, leaving several pieces of silver-beige fur in his wake. Hazel wrinkled her nose and picked up the fluff. She'd never known the cat to shed that much, just the usual stray hairs left on unsuspecting laps like Shrewsbury's. But those were always one or two fine needles of fur, not as many as this. Maybe it was time for a good brushing. Alice would have a fit and fall in it if she found a pile of cat hair like this anywhere near her kitchen. And she and Dickens were just starting to warm to each other too.

As she stared at the fur in her hand, a memory stirred. That first day she'd visited Farnsworth Abbey and looked out the turret room window, there'd been a clump of fur on the roof near the edge of the guttering. Then, later, Mrs. Crosby had said that Doris loved the Wakefields' cat, Norwich, and used to chase him down from trees and rooftops to keep him safe.

Dickens purred loudly as he groomed his paws in the sunshine, and Hazel chuckled. "I'm sure you'd love to climb trees and get on rooftops, wouldn't you?"

As if in response, the feline looked at her, gaze narrowed, then glanced back out the window, scooting away slightly before meowing loudly again and jumping down off the sill. Perhaps her Dickens wasn't a climber like Norwich after all, and for that Hazel was glad. She shuddered at the thought of the cat getting stuck out there on a precarious ledge and her having to go after him to fetch him back.

Hazel straightened as her thoughts screeched to a halt. Wait. Could that have been what happened to poor Doris? Had Norwich gotten out again and she went out on the roof to go get him then slipped and fell by accident? The cat's presence would certainly explain the tuft of black fur she'd seen on the rooftop too.

But that didn't make sense. Several of the staff had mentioned seeing Norwich down on the ground level by Doris's body after she fell. There was no way he could have jumped from a three-story height and survived unscathed, nine lives or not.

And that line of thought still didn't explain the pregnancy corset or the incorrect size.

Hazel slumped back in her chair, toying absently with the clump of Dickens's fur. None of the puzzle pieces fit together like a proper case should, and it was getting irritating. Mrs. Crosby had specifically said she was in the turret room and looked out the window to see Norwich and the other staff members downstairs around Doris's body.

Frowning, she rifled through her drawers to find

the map she'd drawn that day down in the kitchen to show Alice and Maggie where the rooms at Farnsworth Abbey were located. Per her conversation with Betsy earlier, George, Mr. Donovan, and Harrison were already in the turret room when she got there. Mrs. Crosby and Thomas followed up the stairs shortly thereafter.

The only person who hadn't been present and accounted for was Miss Eugenia, but Betsy had said she was in her rooms, not feeling well. She'd said the girl had been sick. Lord Wakefield had an alibi, and Mrs. Crosby passed Mrs. Wakefield coming down the stairs from the turret room and—oh!

"That's it!" she said, snapping her fingers at Dickens to get his attention. "We need to call Inspector Gibson right away. I know who the killer is and the reason behind the murder. And they got it wrong. All wrong!"

## CHAPTER NINETEEN

At four p.m. sharp as they'd arranged, Hazel met Detective Chief Inspector Gibson at Farnsworth Abbey. She figured teatime was as good as any to catch the entire Wakefield household together. Harrison, the butler, answered the door and let them inside then took their coats. Hazel smoothed her hand down the front of her plum-colored day dress then pulled Betsy aside as she scurried past and whispered for her to go up to the attic and search for one thing.

The maid nodded and rushed off.

"You're sure you're ready for this?" Michael asked as the butler led them toward the dining room, where the family was gathered. "You believe that strongly in your hunches? Hunches you've yet to share with me?"

"I do." Hazel nodded, clasping her hands together in front of her to hide their nervous tremble. Her

Charles had always said that catching a criminal was eighty percent facts and fifteen percent instinct—with the other five percent being pure luck—and she was about to prove him right. Harrison announced their arrival, and all the Wakefield family looked up at her and Michael in unison, their expressions shocked, to say the least.

Lord Wakefield was the first to recover, his tone deliberately bland, in direct opposition to his irritated expression. "You again, Chief Inspector? I do hope you've solved the case this time, so we can be done with this nasty business."

Michael looked from the lord to Hazel, his kind brown gaze twinkling mischievously. "Indeed we have. Or should I say, Mrs. Martin here has a theory."

"A theory?" Huffing, Lord Wakefield sat back in his seat and crossed his arms. "Well, spit it out then, Mrs. Martin."

"Well, sir, I believe Doris's murder was somewhat of a misunderstanding," Hazel said.

"A misunderstanding?" The lord's frown darkened. "And what does this misunderstanding have to do with any of us? I was led to believe the death had something to do with that no-good chauffeur of ours disappearing."

"As did we. At first." Hazel glanced at Michael

then turned to Lady Wakefield. "I believe you said you were in your sewing room and your husband was in his study that Thursday night when you heard Doris's scream. Is that correct, Lady Wakefield?"

Lord Wakefield cleared his throat.

"Well." Lady Wakefield's gaze darted to her husband then back to Hazel. "Yes, that's correct. Though by now you know I was mistaken about my husband's location, as he's told you. But as for the rest of it, yes. As I said, I was working on my new shawl."

"Right. And a lovely shawl it is too." Hazel moved to Eugenia next. "And you were in your room when you heard the scream, Eugenia?"

She glanced at her brother then nodded.

"And you, Thomas," Hazel said. "Where were you when all this was happening?"

"I was in the front hallway," he said, setting his teacup down then wiping his mouth. "Just coming back from the garage, actually."

"Ah." Hazel raised a brow at him. "Checking to make sure a certain Alphonse Ash was no longer there?"

"No." Thomas visibly bristled, his posture stiffening and dots of crimson appearing on his pale cheeks. "I have no idea what you mean, Mrs. Martin."

"Really?" She tilted her head. "So you didn't fight

with the chauffeur, as other witnesses have testified, and demand he leave the employ of this house?"

Eugenia pushed to her feet, her pale cheeks flushed now as well. "Thomas did not kill Doris, if that's what you're implying!"

"I'm not implying anything, dear. Please sit down before you make yourself even more unwell," Hazel said, gesturing toward the girl's chair. "Though I will admit your brother was on my suspect list for a while, as were many others. But you see, in the end, I couldn't find one single person on my list who had all three elements—means, motive, and opportunity. But then again, I had the motive part all wrong until today." She glanced around the table and gave a small smile. "As did the killer."

Lord Wakefield stood as well now, grousing. "Just what are you blasted well getting at, Mrs. Martin?" He threw his linen napkin down on the table and glowered at Michael. "Is this completely necessary, Inspector? Since when do you let civilians run around accusing members of the aristocracy of murder?"

"I'm only doing my due diligence here, sir." Michael held up his hands in supplication. "As a public servant. And please, just hear the lady out. She's to be trusted, I swear. After all, she's well bred, and she learned her investigative skills from the best, her late husband."

Warmed by the compliment and bolstered by his confidence, Hazel continued, turning her attention back to Lord Wakefield. "You originally claimed you go to the club on Thursdays, though you were at a different location the night of Doris's murder, weren't you? You were actually across town on Grove Street that night, yes? At Mrs. Pommel's house, correct? The police have verified your alibi, which takes you off the list of suspects."

The lord lowered his head, some of his bluster dissipating under his wife's heated glare. "Yes, I was there. I'm sorry, Constance."

Lady Wakefield huffed and turned away from him, clearly not in a forgiving mood.

"That also means, Lord Wakefield, that you couldn't have been in your study the week before, arguing with Doris, either, because you actually were at the club that week."

He looked back up at Hazel, his expression confused. "That's correct."

Hazel took pity on the beleaguered man whose marriage was crumbling before her very eyes. "Davis, your interim chauffeur, was kind enough to detail your Thursday-evening timetable for me. You alternate your trips to Grove Street with visits to your club, every other week."

Lord Wakefield grunted in acknowledgment then slumped back into his seat.

"And Thomas." She turned to the son next. "Were you in your father's study, arguing with Doris, a week before she died?"

Thomas shook his head, still stunned after the revelation of his father's affair, apparently. "No, madam."

"I'm sorry, but haven't you done enough damage here, Mrs. Martin?" Lady Wakefield dabbed her mouth with a linen napkin then stood, her irritation giving way to full-blown outrage. "You accuse my husband of infidelity, you hurl insults at my children. And still you've yet to get to your point. Please do so now, Mrs. Martin, or I'll be forced to ask you to leave."

Hazel leaned back slightly to glance out into the hall. No sign of Betsy yet, which meant she needed to stall for more time. Michael gave her a get-on-with-it look, which she did her best to ignore as she faced down the table full of Wakefield family members once more.

Sending Betsy up to the attic had been a risk. If the proof she needed wasn't there, it could blow her whole theory. Hazel swallowed hard against the constriction in her dry throat and forced a confident smile she didn't quite feel. "Lady Wakefield, I remember you showing me the beautiful shawl you'd made and explaining how you were lucky enough to be the first to happen upon the silk that had just been delivered by train. You said you bought it from Madam Pinkerton's haberdashery shop?"

"Yes." Lady Wakefield crossed her arms and tapped the toe of her black shoe against the thick Persian carpet. She'd dressed all in black today—the color of loss and mourning—fitting for what was about to happen, Hazel supposed.

"And that shop is directly across from the train station, isn't it? You said yourself that you could see the station clearly through the gigantic plate-glass windows where they display all the new fabric at the front of the shop. I believe it looks directly at the ticket office, isn't that correct, Lady Wakefield?"

Color flushed Lady Wakefield's cheeks, made even more apparent by the somber hue of her clothing, and she glanced at her son before answering. "Yes, I suppose that's true. But I still fail to see your point."

Hazel turned back to Thomas again. "You were at that train station that day, weren't you? Perhaps buying tickets and maybe meeting with someone?"

"What if I was?" He looked away, his face red and

his expression embarrassed. "I certainly did not kill Doris."

"I know you didn't," Hazel said, her gaze narrowed. "On the night of the murder, Mrs. Crosby testified to me and the police that she was in the dining room when she heard Doris's scream and saw Betsy run past the doorway from the library. She followed behind Betsy. At the top of the stairs on the third floor, she met Lady Wakefield heading down. And by that point, Betsy, Mr. Donovan, George, and Harrison were all in the turret room. Mrs. Crosby also reported that you, Thomas, came up the stairs right behind her, which means it would have been impossible for you to kill Doris then have time to run out of the turret room and all the way downstairs without being seen."

"My son would never have killed that maid," Lady Wakefield said, her tone emphatic.

"Agreed," Hazel continued. "The true killer, however, found themselves in a bit of a dilemma. Because Doris's scream sent people running up the stairs almost immediately and because that lone stairway is the only exit from the turret room. Thus, the real murderer was trapped upstairs, unable to get away without being seen."

Lord Wakefield rested his hands on the table and leaned forward, his dark gaze narrowed. "So what you're saying is it must have been someone who was still in the turret room?"

"Well, sir, I did consider that, but it is incorrect." Hazel slowly started walking around the table, passing by the twins first. "You see, there was another place the killer could go and hide to not be seen. The attic."

"Then the killer could only be someone who was not seen in the turret room or on the ground or on the stairs?" Lord Wakefield narrowed his eyes as Hazel brushed by him.

"You are very nearly correct, sir." Hazel glanced toward the dining room door, relieved to see Betsy finally poke her head around the frame. She cocked her head to indicate the maid should wait, and Betsy nodded, stepping back from the door again.

Hazel continued around the table. "I almost didn't solve the case because none of the original suspects could have pushed Doris. Alphonse Ash had moved too far away by then to have made it back in time for the killing. Eugenia was in her room on the other side of the house and also then too far away. Lord Wakefield was not at home at the time of the murder, and Thomas came up the stairs behind Mrs. Crosby, eliminating him as a suspect." She stopped by Lady Wakefield. "But there was one person who was going down the stairs, not up, right after the murder."

Lady Wakefield gasped loudly, her hand fluttering to her chest as she realized the full extent of Hazel's statement. "Now wait just a minute, Mrs. Martin. Whatever are you suggesting? I told you that I was in my sewing room when poor Doris fell. I was nowhere near that turret room."

"Ah, but that's not true, now is it, Lady Wakefield? You couldn't have been where you say you were, you see." Hazel blinked as the woman's pasty complexion slowly mottled an unflattering shade of crimson. "If you *had* been in your sewing room as you'd claimed, then Mrs. Crosby would have either seen you rush past the dining room on your way to the kitchen, or you would have come up the stairs behind her, as Thomas did."

Lady Wakefield stared at Hazel, her mouth flapping to form words that didn't come.

"At first I thought you had lied about being in the sewing room so that you could claim Lord Wakefield was home even though you knew he wasn't. I imagine you didn't want his affair with Mrs. Pommel revealed." Hazel caught the shocked look on Lord Wakefield's face. Had he really thought he could hide something like that from his wife? In Hazel's experience, the wife always knew. She continued, "But now I realize you had another reason."

"Well, I never. That doesn't mean anything," Lady Wakefield hissed. "There was so much confusion that night. No one's entirely sure of who they saw and when or where."

"Ah, but Betsy was entirely confident about exactly who was in the room. You may have been in the turret room earlier, but the maid didn't list you as one of the people she saw there after Doris fell because you *weren't* there. That's because you'd hidden yourself in the attic when you heard all the people rushing upstairs." Hazel glanced back to the dining room door again and nodded for Betsy to enter. "Plus, you had a prop to get rid of as well."

"Prop? What?" The color in Lady Wakefield's cheeks began to drain away, leaving her slightly grey as the maid approached, holding out a bunched-up black sable stole. "That's not a prop. That's my very expensive, ruined fur. This is absurd."

"Not absurd at all. This is what you used to lure Doris out the window isn't it, Lady Wakefield?" Hazel took the item from Betsy. "Funny how it looks almost exactly like Norwich's fur. And you knew Doris had a soft spot for that cat. Mrs. Crosby even told me she put herself in danger, climbing trees and even retrieving him from the gazebo roof. It would have been a simple trick to bunch it up and push it over to the side so one could barely see part of it. It would easily be mistaken for Norwich. Then you simply got Doris to climb out of that third-floor window to rescue the cat she loved. Then, once the maid was on the ledge, you pushed her, poor thing. Afterward, you pulled your stole back inside before anyone could see it."

Hazel ran her fingers through the thick, plush fur, indicating the area where a patch was missing. "Trouble was, you left a bit of evidence behind. There's still a tuft of it stuck on the guttering. That's what finally alerted me to what had happened. Well, that and your conversation with Eugenia about your damaged fur at the restaurant that day." Hazel smiled, small and sad. "Anyway, afterward, you hid this stole in the attic, and when the pound of footsteps on the stairs stopped, you sneaked back out into the hallway, thinking the coast was clear. I imagine you'd thought you'd just rejoin the people in the turret room and pretend you'd also just come up the stairs. But it didn't work out that way, did it? Unfortunately for you, Mrs. Crosby and Thomas were almost at the landing, and you couldn't risk them seeing you enter the room from the wrong end of the hallway, so you panicked and made for the staircase instead to make it look as if you'd already been in the turret room and were now leaving."

Jaw tense, Lady Wakefield gave a derisive snort. "Well, that's a very entertaining tale, Mrs. Martin. You've forgotten one very important detail, however. I have no motive whatsoever. Why in the world would I want to kill that poor maid?"

Hazel glanced up at Michael and saw his slight nod, so she continued. "Actually, you did have a good reason for wanting the maid gone, one very important to you. You've always been extremely concerned about the tarnishing of your family name. You've told me yourself on several occasions that you had your sights set on a marriage between Thomas and the Tewkes-bury girl and wanted to match your Eugenia up with an earl this season. Having your beloved son involved with one of your household staff was bad enough. Then the fact you thought he'd got the girl pregnant and was going to run away with her by train was completely unacceptable."

A chorus of loud gasps filled the dining room, from family and staff alike.

Michael's eyes widened slightly at the mention of the pregnancy that wasn't real, but Hazel prayed he trusted her enough to go with it. Luckily, he watched her closely but remained silent.

She turned back to Lady Wakefield. "At least, I imagine that's what you thought when you saw the receipt that was delivered here from Etienne's a few days later, right? After all, you said you sort through all the household mail. And after glimpsing your son and Doris conspiring together at the train station the day you bought the new silk material for that shawl, you must have fit those pieces together into a tidy, if false, puzzle."

"No! I—" Lady Wakefield gripped the edge of the table tight, her knuckles white. "I swear I never—"

"Don't bother denying you saw them, Lady Wakefield," Hazel said, halting her protest. "But you see, their meeting at the station that day wasn't what you thought. They weren't conspiring to elope together. Quite the contrary, in fact."

Lady Wakefield visibly deflated at those words, cracking at last, as her shoulders slumped and her head lowered. "That little floozy was only after my family's money. At that stage, I wouldn't have put anything past her."

"You even tried to bribe Doris, didn't you?" Hazel said, rounding on the woman again. "It was you she argued with in Lord Wakefield's study a week before her death, wasn't it?"

"If she'd only taken my offer, then she'd still be alive."

"Doris refused your money, though, didn't she?"

Hazel said, her throat dry and her pulse pounding from adrenaline. She felt like Detective Archibald Fox in her books at that exhilarating moment when all the clues fell into place perfectly. "She refused because she was innocent of all the horrible things you'd accused her of. You shoved an innocent maid, sending her plummeting to her death."

"You're wrong," Lady Wakefield said, her tone now desperate as she backed toward the wall, her gaze darting between the other people in the room. "Our family would've been ruined because of that girl and her bastard child."

"Wrong again, I'm afraid, Lady Wakefield," Hazel said, feeling almost sorry for the woman. Almost. "You see, it was never Doris who was pregnant."

"What?" Pressed against the wall, Lady Wakefield was visibly shaking now. "But—"

"Mother," Eugenia sobbed, "is it true that you pushed her? Doris was my friend."

"I was only trying to protect this family, protect you, from that gold digger."

"No! She was never after our money. She was a good person." Eugenia swiped the tears from her cheeks, anger sparking hot in her pale-blue eyes, her spirit rallying at last. "And Mrs. Martin is right. It wasn't Doris who was pregnant, Mother. It's me. I'm pregnant. By Alphonse Ash, who ran out on me right after I told him. Doris was only trying to help me out."

Another gasp echoed through the room, and Hazel gave Michael a knowing look.

"It's true," Eugenia continued. "That's why my brother fought with him. He did it on my behalf to get him to own up to his responsibilities."

Lady Wakefield's face crumpled with disgust. "The chauffeur is the father of your baby?"

"Yes, he is. I loved him." Eugenia squared her shoulders and lifted her chin, looking calm and confident for the first time in Hazel's recollection. "It was never my intention to ruin the family name, but I thought he cared for me too. Once he made it clear he had no interest in our child, I was hoping to leave before anyone found out about my condition. Doris and I were going to run away up north so I could have the baby in private, and then she was going to bring up the child as hers. Thomas was helping us make the arrangements."

"Oh, my dear." Lady Wakefield rushed around the table and took her daughter's stiff form into her arms, having an apparent about-face—or a last attempt to elicit clemency for herself. "I'm so sorry this happened to you. I had no idea. A grandchild?" She squeezed her daughter tight then looked at Michael and Hazel over the girl's shoulder. "Though I imagine I'll never get to see him or her now, since you'll arrest me."

Michael cleared his throat, glancing at Hazel, who nudged him toward the guilty party. "Uh, yes. I'm sorry, madam. But I'm afraid I must take you down to the station. You are hereby under arrest for the murder of Doris Carmichael..."

As he stepped forward to take Lady Wakefield into custody, Hazel glanced down to find Norwich by her feet, meowing loudly as he watched Lady Wakefield with his knowing green eyes. Apparently, Dickens wasn't the only feline who could sniff out murder.

## CHAPTER TWENTY

---

Three days later, Hazel was back in the kitchen at Hastings Manor. Alice, Maggie, Duffy, Shrewsbury, and Michael were all gathered around the table with her, and they were enjoying Alice's latest treat du jour.

"How's that Madeira cake, Inspector Gibson?" Alice asked.

"Delicious, as always," Michael said around a large mouthful. "Thank you."

Alice blushed profusely at the compliment, and Hazel had to smile. It seemed her cook was so smitten with the inspector she'd failed to notice Dickens sneaking into the room. The cat twined around Hazel's ankles, and she scooped him up onto her lap, scratching behind his ears.

"Well, it looks like you were proven right in the

end, Maggie," she said. "Your friend Doris really was a nice girl."

"Yes, madam." The maid smiled. "Thank you for clearing her name. I knew you would."

"What I still don't understand, though, is how you finally knew it was Lady Wakefield," Alice said. "All from one clump of dark fur."

Hazel kissed the top of Dickens's head and smiled. "I'm actually embarrassed how long it took me. That clue was there from day one. All I really needed to do was just see things in a different way."

"How so?" Duffy asked.

"Well, for so long, I was fixated on the idea that someone wanted to kill Doris because of her pregnancy. Later, when we found out there was no baby, then I assumed she must have been faking the whole thing for monetary gain. I even made the false assumption that she'd bought that pregnancy corset for herself, when in reality, she'd been buying it for Eugenia. That also explains why it was too big."

"I don't know, madam," Alice said, shaking her head. "Still seems like an awfully big chance for Lady Wakefield to take."

"Not really, Alice. When you consider how concerned she is with appearances and her family name." Hazel shrugged and glanced at Michael, who was finished with his slab of cake. "Her pride clouded her judgment. And she most likely thought the police wouldn't pay much attention to the death, since Doris was only a maid. Turns out she was wrong about that, thankfully."

Michael wiped his mouth with a napkin then pushed his empty plate away. "And that was her second mistake. We do our best to treat every victim with the same urgency, no matter their class or profession. At least I do. Perhaps not all the detective inspectors are quite as diligent."

"What was her first mistake, besides killing Doris?" Hazel asked him, curious.

He winked at her and smiled. "Letting you into Farnsworth Abbey that first day to snoop around."

Heat prickled her cheeks at the warmth in his eyes, and she quickly focused on Dickens instead. "Well, she did go to great lengths to make Doris's death appear to be a suicide too," Hazel added. "She even primed Mrs. Crosby with those thoughts and assured her she should talk to the police about them."

"Lucky for us she never counted on you digging into the case as well, madam," Maggie said, grinning with pride. "You solved it all." The maid glanced at Michael, and her eyes widened slightly. "Oh, and you too, of course, Detective Chief Inspector Gibson."

Chuckles filled the air from around the table until Shrewsbury cleared his throat.

Maggie looked at him too, crimson flushing her cheeks. "And you as well, Shrewsbury!"

Laughing, Hazel continued. "Anyway, once I realized that Lady Wakefield would have seen the receipt that was delivered from Lady Etienne's, it sparked the idea. She'd been so proud to tell me she personally handled all the mail and deliveries for the Farnsworth household that first day I'd gone to the abbey. Then, when I saw a clump of hair Dickens here had shed, it was just a matter of connecting the dots. After discussing that cloth for the shawl with her, I knew it was likely from the haberdashery's location that she'd seen Doris and Thomas at the train station together that day she was buying her silk. They were seen together by someone else and it's likely she saw them too. Add in the fact she *wasn't* in the turret room when Betsy got there, and the conversation I'd overheard between her and her daughter that day at the restaurant, and it all became clear."

"Imagine," Alice said, shaking her head. "And she was the one Betsy heard Doris arguing with in the study that day too."

"Yes." Hazel put a squirming Dickens down on the floor. "We knew it couldn't have been Lord Wakefield, since it was already confirmed that he'd been across town at Mrs. Pommel's that night. But it had to have been a member of the Wakefield family, since two servants wouldn't have risked being in the study alone. And it didn't make sense for Thomas to fight with her, given we thought he and Doris were lovers and he'd already scared off Alphonse Ash." She shrugged. "And Doris and Eugenia were friends. The only other person left was Lady Wakefield. It made sense that she would try to buy Doris off to keep her from sinking her claws into Thomas and the Wakefield fortune."

"But Doris was too loyal to Eugenia to accept her bribe," Maggie said.

Michael sat back and crossed his arms, narrowing his gaze on Hazel. "I noticed you let Lord Wakefield's little secret out of the bag."

Hazel frowned. "You mean about him going to Grove Street instead of his club every other Thursday?" She sniffed. "Well, honestly, I didn't see a way around it. And it was time for all of the Wakefields to come clean about their secrets, anyway."

"How did you figure out it was Eugenia who was pregnant, madam?" Alice asked.

"Things didn't add up. Why would Thomas and Alphonse argue like that? If it was over Doris, then that meant Thomas had won, he'd run Alphonse off, and therefore had no reason to kill Doris in a fit of rage. On the other hand, Alphonse couldn't have killed Doris either, since he was too far away at the time. Besides, Eugenia had been acting so strangely. Plus, she was deathly pale and not eating. She seemed unusually nervous too, when I mentioned Doris's trip. I remembered Alice mentioning that day when we made the tarts about knowing someone who went away to have her baby and the sister brought up the child. I figured why couldn't Eugenia and Doris have a similar arrangement? If Doris raised the baby, Eugenia could avoid bringing shame on the family name, and she could still help support Doris and her child in secret."

"What about the baby's father? Alphonse?" Alice asked. "They found him, right? Is he going to be made to take responsibility?"

"Yes, I found him," Shrewsbury said. "But he wants no part in the child's life, sadly. Probably for the best, since I don't think he'll be working...or much else for a while."

At the odd comment, Hazel raised a brow at her butler, but he remained silent. He was wearing white gloves tonight too, which wasn't a usual part of his wardrobe. She remembered his ominous threats from earlier regarding the missing chauffeur and had a feeling Shrewsbury had taken matters into his own hands. Literally. Well, she couldn't say she blamed the man. Alphonse needed to learn there were consequences for his actions, no matter how harsh.

"Eugenia's better off without him, in my opinion," Michael said. "Lady Wakefield still seems enamored with the idea of a grandchild, despite all the troubles ahead of her. Hard to tell if it's just an act to gain sympathy for her trial or not, but I suspect so considering she didn't seem quite as enamored when she thought the grandchild was the product of her son and a lowly maid. And Thomas seemed quite supportive and prepared to stand behind Eugenia and her baby through everything. Even Lord Wakefield seems to have softened toward his daughter and her predicament. She doesn't need the likes of Alphonse Ash." Michael hiked his chin. "She told me she's naming the baby after Doris, if it's a girl."

"Too bad Lady Wakefield will only be able to enjoy her first grandchild from a prison cell," Alice said. "But I guess that's no more than she deserves, after what she did."

"No one's above the law." Michael looked at Hazel. "She took a life and has to pay the price."

"Well, I say job well done all around," Maggie said. "Here's to lessons learned."

"Indeed." Hazel smiled and raised her teacup in a toast to her staff. "And new friends made. I have all of you to thank. Michael and I couldn't have solved this mystery without you."

"Hear! Hear!" Duffy toasted everyone with his mug then grinned. "So, when's our next case?"

\*\*\*\*\*\*\*\*\*

READ MORE BOOKS in this series:

*Murder at Lowry House (book 1)*

SIGN UP TO join my email list to get all my latest release at the lowest possible price, plus as a benefit for signing up today, I will send you a copy of a Leighann Dobbs book that hasn't been published anywhere...yet!

http://www.leighanndobbs.com/newsletter

IF YOU ARE ON FACEBOOK, please join my VIP readers group and get exclusive content plus updates on all my books. It's a fun group where you can feel at home, ask questions and talk about your favorite reads:

https://www.facebook.com/groups/ldobbsreaders/

IF YOU WANT to receive a text message on your cell phone when I have a new release, text COZYMYS-TERY to 88202 (sorry, this only works for US cell phones!)

## Cozy Mysteries

### *Hazel Martin Historical Mystery Series*

\*\*\*

*Murder at Lowry House (book 1)*

*Murder by Misunderstanding (book 2)*

-------

### *Regency Matchmaker Mysteries*

\*\*\*

*An Invitation to Murder (Book 1)*

-------

## Sam Mason Mysteries

## (As L. A. Dobbs)

\*\*\*

Telling Lies (Book 1)

Keeping Secrets (Book 2)

Exposing Truths (Book 3)

--------

## *Lexy Baker Cozy Mystery Series*

\* \* \*

*Lexy Baker Cozy Mystery Series Boxed Set Vol 1 (Books 1-4)*

*Or buy the books separately:*

*Killer Cupcakes*

*Dying For Danish*

*Murder, Money and Marzipan*

*3 Bodies and a Biscotti*

*Brownies, Bodies & Bad Guys*

*Bake, Battle & Roll*

*Wedded Blintz*

*Scones, Skulls & Scams*

*Ice Cream Murder*

*Mummified Meringues*

*Brutal Brulee (Novella)*

*No Scone Unturned*

*Cream Puff Killer*

-------

## *Mooseamuck Island Cozy Mystery Series*

\* \* \*

*A Zen For Murder*

*A Crabby Killer*

*A Treacherous Treasure*

-------

## *Silver Hollow*

## *Paranormal Cozy Mystery Series*

\*\*\*

A Spell of Trouble (Book 1)

Spell Disaster (Book 2)

Nothing to Croak About (Book 3)

Cry Wolf (Book 4)

-------

## *Mystic Notch*

## Cat Cozy Mystery Series

* * *

*Ghostly Paws*

*A Spirited Tail*

*A Mew To A Kill*

*Paws and Effect*

*Probable Paws*

-------

## Blackmoore Sisters
## Cozy Mystery Series

* * *

*Dead Wrong*

*Dead & Buried*

*Dead Tide*

*Buried Secrets*

*Deadly Intentions*

*A Grave Mistake*

*Spell Found*

*Fatal Fortune*

-------

# Magical Romance with a Touch of Mystery

### ***

*Something Magical*

*Curiously Enchanted*

-------

# Romantic Comedy

### ***

## Corporate Chaos Series

*In Over Her Head (book 1)*

*Can't Stand the Heat (book 2)*

-------

# Contemporary Romance

### ***

*Reluctant Romance*

-------

# Sweet Romance (Written As Annie Dobbs)

*Hometown Hearts Series*

**\*\*\***

*No Getting Over You* (Book 1)

*A Change of Heart* (Book 2)

-------

**\*\*\***

**Sweetrock Sweet and Spicy Cowboy Romance**

*Some Like It Hot*

*Too Close For Comfort*

----

**Regency Romance**

\* \* \*

**Scandals and Spies Series:**

*Kissing The Enemy*

*Deceiving the Duke*

*Tempting the Rival*

*Charming the Spy*

*Pursuing the Traitor*

**The Unexpected Series:**

*An Unexpected Proposal*

*An Unexpected Passion*

**Dobbs Fancytales:**

Dobbs Fancytales Boxed Set Collection

———

**Western Historical Romance**

**\*\*\***

**Goldwater Creek Mail Order Brides:**

*Faith*

**American Mail Order Brides Series:**

Chevonne: Bride of Oklahoma

------------------

**ROMANTIC SUSPENSE**

**WRITING AS LEE ANNE JONES:**

**\*\*\***

**The Rockford Security Series:**

Deadly Betrayal (Book 1)

Fatal Games (Book 2)

Treacherous Seduction (Book 3)

Calculating Desires (Book 4)

Wicked Deception (Book 5)

# ABOUT THE AUTHOR

USA Today bestselling author, Leighann Dobbs, discovered her passion for writing after a twenty year career as a software engineer. She lives in New Hampshire with her husband Bruce, their trusty Chihuahua mix Mojo and beautiful rescue cat, Kitty. When she's not reading, gardening, making jewelry or selling antiques, she likes to write cozy mystery and historical romance books.

Her book "Dead Wrong" won the "Best Mystery Romance" award at the 2014 Indie Romance Convention.

Her book "Ghostly Paws" was the 2015 Chanticleer Mystery & Mayhem First Place category winner in the Animal Mystery category.

Find out about her latest books by signing up at:


http://www.leighanndobbs.com/newsletter


Connect with Leighann on Facebook
http://facebook.com/leighanndobbsbooks


Join her VIP readers group on Facebook:
https://www.facebook.com/groups/ldobbsreaders
/

45802963R00126

Made in the USA
San Bernardino, CA
01 August 2019